Books by Reneé Porter

Bell Park

The Dreamville Trilogy
Dreamville
Gordon's Dreams
Pieces of April

The Taliaferro Chronicles
The 13th Victim
Redemption Ridge
An Inquisition of Angels

Pieces of April

Dreamville III

Reneé Porter

Roet Press   Plantation, Florida

DEDICATION

For Rob, who taught me to love.
I would cross worlds for you, too

PROLOGUE

Will first saw the boy at Pamela's funeral. He glanced at the large window reflecting the brightly lit room against the black mirror of night and saw a boy standing there. When he turned to look where the boy should have been in the room, he saw no one. But, when he looked back to the window the boy was still there, standing alone and staring directly at Will.

Will closed his eyes and sighed, wanting the evening to end. He felt as if the event in his home was tricking his eyes. There was no boy in the room, but yet there he stood reflected in the window.

Instead of going to the window, he walked to where Pamela's friends from college were gathered. When he was away, Pamela went to them. She thought he was ignorant of her little escapes, but he knew. When she was lonely or tired or sad, she went to them. She had submitted to him willingly in their marriage, but they, they were given her every secret.

He hated them for it. He hated them for living and he hated her for dying and leaving him alone. He wanted them to leave. Pamela's death was his pain, his loss, not theirs. How could they understand that in Pamela he had found a woman completely submissive?

He had always been cool to those friends before the marriage and had kept her from them after. He had always felt that he should have been enough for her and he resented any intrusion into his marriage. Had it really mattered that he seldom spoke or wanted to hear her trivial comments on things that meant nothing to him? That they were together was all that was important. The rest of it was simply white noise, the constant hum of distant radios and televisions which only broke the perfect silence of how he wanted their marriage to be. It took time to cure her of her waste of his time with her chatter. At first she had been hurt, but the she gave in finally when one night at supper he had waved his hand at her and without looking at her, simply declared, "I've no time for your ceaseless chatter.

Enough."

No, it should not have mattered. He was there. Why hadn't that been enough for her? It was for him. He gave her a home. He married her and loved her in the only way he knew how. Nothing else should have mattered.

No, it did not matter, especially now that she was gone. He sat with her friends, but said nothing and did not listen to anything they said. They bored him. He could not imagine how they had ever had anything to say to each other that could have interested her.

He looked around the room and realized that the only people there for him were people who either worked with him or for him. In other words, people only slightly different than the fools he was suffering now.

He had no family or friends there. Pamela had been his only family. No siblings or cousins and his parents had died long ago. There were a few neighbors there whose names he could barely remember. But no one else.

He looked back to the window and the boy was still there. He peered into the night behind the boy and could see candlelight. Turning again to the room around him, he still did not see the boy and certainly not candlelight.

He shook his head as if to shrug off the vision. He had

to regain control of his senses. Pamela was dead. He would get through the evening and then tomorrow return to work and move on with his life. He was still young and no longer chained to a woman he had thought was intelligent because she was well read. If he would need companionship in the future, he would find it in one of the women who were always around him. He didn't need a wife, but Pamela's absence was affecting him nevertheless and that made him impatiently angry.

He tried not to think of how different life would be without her there waiting for him. He truthfully had only thought of her existence within the framework of his own life. He could not imagine that she might have had a life outside the one they shared. He married her because she matched every parameter he required in a wife, from her family and breeding to her looks and education. He never considered that she might have her own needs and desires in their relationship.

After the wedding, when she began to assert herself, he quashed those tendencies quickly. He broke her spirit without ever laying a hand on her. Instead of physically breaking her, he ridiculed her at every chance, never spoke of her beauty or intelligence, and belittled her family as often as possible, especially her mother's small business. He tried every way he could think of to make her think that her family was inferior to him. By the time two years had passed, she had become the docile creature he needed as a wife – a woman who lived only when she served his own purposes.

But the one time she had disregarded his wishes was the last time he had seen her. If she had given him the chance to tell her that she had to stay home while he went to the club and played tennis, she would be alive. It was her fault she was dead. She had decided to go to her family's home. She had decided to stay the night there and left him to dine alone at the club. He had come home to find the police waiting at his door. It was not his fault she made a stupid mistake and found herself tortured and shot during a home invasion at her parent's house. Her mistake had ended her life and had inconvenienced him enormously.

If she had been a good wife and stayed home with him, made his dinner, and sat with him, she would not be dead and he would not have to continue listening to these inane voices around him.

Damn, he thought as he looked up, the brat was still in the window. He walked to the window and touched it.

The glass shimmered and felt like the surface skin of a pool of water. He jerked his hand from it as if it had emitted a static electric shock. He stared at his long fingers and the glass in surprise. Then he looked back at the reflection again and for a moment and he could see behind the boy. He could see several people standing there. And one of them was his dead wife. He jerked his head in the direction of where they would be standing in the room, but still saw no one there.

He pushed at the glass, but this time it did not move or shimmer. The reflection grew dimmer and the people in the room behind him began to fill up the void left where the boy and Pamela and another person stood.

He started to call out her name and then stopped himself, pressing his hands against the sides of his legs, taking deep breaths to regain control of himself.

An illusion. A need to see Pamela a last time, though he realized that she didn't look like his wife as his wife had looked before she had died. The Pamela he saw was far too young to have been his wife.

He could feel his face reddening in anger. Damn her. Damn her immortal soul for dying and leaving him alone. And damn her for torturing his mind with illusions of her as a young woman. Damn her. Damn her. Damn her.

Chapter One

Gordon Stewart flung open the doors to Burnock of the future, praying that he had returned from Dreamville to his present time. He prayed that the illusion of April's gravestone was a warning and not a reality where he was stuck. When he saw his cousin Sheila descending the staircase, still a young woman, he almost fell to his knees. He was back. April still lived. He found it difficult to breathe and grasped the door to hold himself up. It was only when he looked down at his hand that he realized how wrong he was. Instead of seeing his young, firm hand, he saw instead a pale, dry and age-spotted thin hand.

The young woman who looked so much like his cousin Sheila ran to him and took him by the elbow, leading him into the parlor.

"Uncle Gordon, I know today is always difficult for you, but you really shouldn't go out there in this weather. It's not healthy for you."

Gordon looked to the girl and smiled sadly. Sheila and Andrew's daughter, Emily. She would be this old now. A beautiful young woman who reminded him so much of her mother – kind and gentle. He supposed that Sheila had never told Emily of Dreamville. He couldn't imagine Andrew ever agreeing to allow it.

Gordon leaned back against the settee and glanced around the room. It had become so shabby. He supposed that he had not changed it since the date on the gravestone. He wondered if he had not had staff to keep it clean if it would have looked like Mrs. Havisham's mouldering home in *Great Expectations*. Above his head, he could see that the plaster which had needed repair in his reality had now completely disintegrated leaving pale ghosts of where it had once been now staining the paint on the ceiling.

He placed one hand across his eyes and quietly laughed to himself at what he had allowed to become of his life in this Dreamville iteration.

"Uncle Gordon, are you alright?"

He moved his hand from his eyes, patted Emily on the

shoulder and smiled.

"I'm fine, young lady. The cold isn't kind on my joints. But you should go home. Assure your parents I will be fine. I'm sure you have friends you'd rather be spending time with them rather than an old man in a falling down house."

Emily stared at him and then lowered her head.

"Uncle Gordon, father died seven years ago. I think today is harder than you think. Do you want me to call mother? Would you rather see her?"

Gordon sighed. Damn, he thought. Andrew was dead. Well, how the hell was he supposed to know? He had never travelled here before. The only reason he recognized Emily was her resemblance to Sheila that had continued from her childhood. And even then she had been a sweet child.

"No, no. Emily, I want you to go back home and be assured that I will be fine. Yes, today is difficult, but I'll be fine. Trust me. Now off with you and give a good report to your lovely mother."

Emily stood and squeezed Gordon's hand lightly.

"I suppose if you promise to stay out of the weather I'll head back to Edinburgh. And you're right. Bryan will be glad to have me home. I'm sure the baby is wearing his patience down by now."

She leaned over and kissed Gordon's cheek and went back upstairs to get her valise.

This time he did grin. Sheila was a grandmother. He wondered about the baby, but knew that Sheila must be happy.

He thought about children and imagined that in the short year he and April had had after Alex's death that they had not had children. He couldn't say why he was so sure, but he felt it. He would have given anything to have had a child with her and he grieved as much for their lost children as for their lost life together.

He could hear Emily descending the staircase again and he quickly wiped the corners of his eyes so that she would not be concerned and feel compelled to stay with him. She meant well. He knew that she did, but he also knew that no one or nothing could ease the pain he was feeling now except for returning to his own reality and away from this potential future that Dreamville was revealing to him.

He saw Emily to her car, waved her away, and stood in the doorway looking to the family cemetery. He had never travelled anywhere in Dreamville that April did not exist. He could not fathom why he had travelled here other than to prevent her death. No other reason seemed even remotely rational to him. She was always with him, even in Dreamville from the time they were teenagers, and so where was she now? What future had she been sent to? The idea that she was not there, that she might actually be dead, was almost more than he could bear.

He closed the heavy front doors against the cold Highland winds that swept around Burnock and walked back upstairs, his knees aching from the biting cold that seemed to creep inside the house and into his bones.

His bedroom was unchanged as was the rest of the house. When he had run from the yellow bedroom where April had stayed, he had dropped her black dress in his haste. He picked up the dress and sat on the edge of the bed staring at it. He felt so tired from the shock of the transition to Dreamville and from missing April that he laid back on the bed where they had loved one another and he closed his eyes. Maybe if I sleep, he thought, I will find her sleeping next to me when I wake.

No, he felt he could not leave this Dreamville fast enough.

But he awoke hours later, still in the future Dreamville with April's dress clutched to his chest. He could see the setting sun and wondered if anyone would notice if he just disappeared. Everyone he had loved most in this world had been stolen from him in a single breath and he knew he could not bear to live the life that stretched before him. He was surprised that he had accepted her death as his presence here seemed to indicate. What had kept him alive for almost 25 years without her?

But then, he thought, this is Dreamville and nothing ever made much sense there.

Was April's family still in America? He thought of Rick and Lisa and their child David that had existed in one frame set of Dreamville. Had that timeline continued or had April's death here changed that?

He had so many questions and no answers. He carefully folded the black dress and placed it back on the pillow. If there were answers anywhere, they might be found in his study.

Grumbling from his stomach interrupted his thoughts and he had no idea if he had eaten today. He knew he had to find out where April was and that the answers could be in the study, but something else told him that if he did not eat, he would suffer from it. He felt extraordinarily tired and again knew that it had something more to do with his heath here than April's absence.

Instead if going to the study, he walked back through the silent house to the kitchen where the housekeeper was stirring a copper pot full of lamb stew. He thought of eating lamb stew with April in the village and winced. That had been a good day. He had loved her so much that day. He could close his eyes and see her beautiful, bright smile lighting the day.

Anguish filled him. What if he could not go back? What if this was his reality forever? He sat down at the long kitchen table and the woman cooking looked at him in surprise.

"Sir, you hae na eaten and you need to take your medicine first."

She moved from the stove to the large restaurant refrigerator and removed a small bottle from it. Before he knew it, she had efficiently placed in front of him a plastic wrapped sterile needle, alcohol wipe, and a vial of insulin.

He was surprised. He was diabetic? It was not something he had expected, but it would explain his weight loss and his weakness. His grandfather had been diabetic and it had killed him. Gordon held the vial and the needle in his hand and stared at them. He had no idea how much he was supposed to take or even how to inject it. He almost laughed, thinking of what a great doctor his father had been and how little he himself knew of medicine.

The maid watched the confusion on his face and returned back to his side, taking the needle and placing the insulin in it.

"Sir, you'll hae to raise your sweater."

He silently acceded to her request and barely felt the tiny needle pierce his skin after she had wiped his side with the alcohol pad.

Embarrassment filled him and he could feel his face redden.

"I'm sorry. It's been a bad day," he said.

She did not speak, sparing him further embarrassment, but after disposing of the medical waste and returning the insulin to the refrigerator, she went back to the stove and filled a bowl with the rich stew and placed it in front of him and then poured a large glass of milk for him and added it to his place setting.

"Aye, tis always bad this day, but you'll feel more like yourself after a meal and a good night's sleep. I'm going over to feed my Craig his evening meal, sir. I'll clean up afterward."

Gordon nodded as if he were a child being instructed by his nanny. He wondered about so many things in this life. If he stayed here any longer, he would have to call Sheila. He was then struck by the thought that perhaps in this Dreamville, Sheila had no knowledge of his past reality. If that were true, how could he explain his lack of knowledge of his own life to her?

He finished the stew and made his way to his study. He was shocked to find the door to it locked, not just the latch itself, but also by a chain with a large keyed padlock.

What the hell, he thought? He went back to the kitchen and looked for the house keys. On the key rack, the hook labeled study was empty. He thought of following the maid to ask her and her Craig about the locks, but decided they would think him mad. He went through some of the kitchen doors before he found a large spanner than he might be able to pry the chain from the door. If that failed, he would take an axe to the door if necessary. The lock left him bewildered and something told him that some dark secret was beyond that door and to walk away, but he could not. April's existence outside of Dreamville might depend on what was beyond that chained door.

He wedged the spanner between the door and the

locked chain, tightened it the fit the chain, and felt the old nails holding the chain to the door frame begin to give as he heard the wood splintering. By the time the chain fell the floor, his body was drenched in sweat and he was surprised by how much effort his labors had cost his body. He might not be 26 here, but his mind still felt he was. It was difficult to accept that he was an aging and ill man.

Once the chain was gone, he still could not get the door open and in frustration began to bash at the brass door handle. He had to get into that room.

It was then that the maid returned, running with "her Craig" following close behind her.

"Sir, nae. Not there. You said never there when you threw the keys into the burn years ago."

Gordon straightened his posture and faced them both full on.

"I'm fine, so if you don't mind, I'd prefer to do this alone."

Craig moved to Gordon and nodded his understanding.

"I retrieved the keys from the burn when you threw them in. I thought one day you might want them back."

He handed Gordon the key to the door.

Craig took the maid by the arm and led her away, again leaving Gordon alone in this bewildering world he lived.

Now that he had the key, he was not sure whether to open the door or not. The sense of foreboding returned, but he ignored it and slowly unlocked the door and opened it.

He wasn't quite sure what to expect to find in the study. Other than a great amount of dust and cobwebs, the room looked much as it had when he had last entered it. He turned the switch on the desk lamp, but the bulb had long ago stopped working. By the dim window light, he saw newspapers covering the desktop. Local papers. Tabloids from Edinburgh and London. Even an old edition of *The Times* bearing a date a few days after the one on April's gravestone.

He brushed the dust off the leather chair with a handkerchief from his trouser pocket and sat down to begin to read about his past.

The Times was folded to a yellowed page with a very short notice about the death of his April, noting her American heritage and that she was survived by her husband, the son of the Laird of Burnock as well as her American family. The notice gave no clue as to the nature of her death.

He shoved it aside as well as the Edinburgh paper and the village paper which said almost the same things except for adding more information about the schedule for services.

Last, but certainly not least, were the more brittle and almost crumbling tabloids. He feared those the most as he was unsure whether their articles would include information that was factual rather than pure supposition or fantasy.

The papers were in pieces. The acidic wood pulp they had been printed on had turned a deep yellow, but even with the discoloration he could see the faces in the photographs. In one issue, someone had actually slipped into the private services at the estate and had taken pictures of him surrounded by his and April's families.

He appeared to be a crushed man in those photographs. The grief the photographer had captured suddenly felt as raw and fresh as it must have been to the version of him in the photo. In an inset next to the picture of the family was a small informal photograph of April. She looked just as she had in the days before Alex's death – young, vibrant and so happy.

His eyes wandered across the page from the painful photographs to the headline across the top of the page. He gasped when he read it and carefully turned the pages to find the accompanying article. It could not be, he thought. Never. He felt the crushing pain of Dreamville breaking his spirit and a tightening in his chest.

According to the article, it seemed that they had married the week after Alex's funeral, but instead of returning to the states, they had decided to stay at Burnock. There was a rather snide comment about their precipitous rush to the altar, but he knew their fear of what might happen could have been the only reason why he and April would have married quickly and cared little as to what the writer of the article thought. They had been so afraid of the nightmares Dreamville had given them before that they would have married in an effort to stave off their fears and perhaps change the future Dreamville offered them.

The paper went on to report that after the wedding, April had driven her family back to the airport at Edinburgh, had seen them depart and had never been seen again. She had simply vanished from the earth.

The article went on to say that the police had inspected every possible clue, including security footage of the entire airport. April had been last seen standing and waving goodbye to her family and then was just not there. There was no video of her leaving the airport or even speaking to anyone else there. No car was found. It was only many months later, after the turn of the new year that a woman's skeletal arm had been found just outside of Edinburgh. April's engagement and wedding rings had been found on the fingers of the remains and the police declared her dead.

Gordon checked the date on the paper and saw that it, too, was dated shortly after the Times. He swept the desk clear of the papers and wanted to scream. He had only had one more week with her and not the year he had thought they had by the date on the stone.

He looked down at the papers he had strewn across the floor and saw another article on the search and discovery of April's few remains. One article remarked that if Gordon had not been at Burnock with Sheila and Andrew, he would have been the chief suspect in her murder.

Why would he have let her drive her parents to Edinburgh when she barely knew the roads around Burnock, he asked himself. The memory of her comments of being afraid of the Highland roads was fresh in his mind. She had told him of how afraid she was the day she drove Alex back from the village. He found it impossible to believe that she would have attempted the trip to Edinburgh and back alone so soon.

Why hadn't Ferguson driven them to the airport? So many questions and none of the facts of the account of her disappearance made any sense. He leaned back into the leather chair and stared out the window where he had once thought he had thrown Charlotte.

Another paradox, he thought. Where were Will and Charlotte? One of them was always lurking about in his excursions to Dreamville. He stood and began to pace around the room. As he stopped next to the long disused fireplace, he happened to notice a yellowed envelope. He pulled it from behind the mantel clock and found it contained photographs. Wedding photographs.

They had married in the small family chapel with fewer than 20 guests, almost all family with the exception of Sean and the staff members. He sat down in the old Queen Anne chair and heard the fabric of the chair splitting from age, but he ignored it. He was too engrossed in the pictures in the envelope.

He pulled one of April standing in the garden next to a small bench as she waited for her father to escort her across the lawn to the chapel. To say that she was beautiful was an understatement. He had never seen her look so gloriously happy in his life. She had worn his great grandmother's 1918 ivory wedding gown, her gorgeous mane of dark curls crowned by a ring of fresh flowers. The emptiness he had felt throughout the day disappeared with seeing her lovely features frozen in a solitary moment of such happiness.

Outside the evening was finally turning dark and he heard soft footfalls in the hallway outside the study.

"She was a true beauty, sir," the maid said.

Gordon smiled sadly and nodded in agreement. He stood and removed the study key from his pocket and handed it to her.

"It's alright. I'm going to leave the room unlocked. Perhaps tomorrow you and Craig could help me sort through this ancient mess."

The woman smiled softly and murmured her assent. As she left she reminded him to have a "wee bite" before bed and that she had left some biscuits in the tin on the long kitchen table.

Gordon left shortly after she did and made his way to his bedroom. He closed the door between his room and the yellow bedroom. If this was his life, he would have to learn to live with it and himself. He laid the photographs on the bed table and before climbing into bed and shutting off the light, he returned April's smile of so many years ago.

Chapter Two

Gordon did not wake in the future Dreamville. He awoke alone in his New York bed. He looked across the room to the mirror on the wall and saw that he was young again. Where was he now? Where was April?

He saw his 25 year old face in the mirror and shook his head. It was starting to seem that he needed a mirror to discover exactly where or when he was anymore.

He felt as if he had fallen backward, but was more than happy to be young again where April might still be alive. Perhaps there was a silver lining to this version of Dreamville. He only prayed that Charlotte was not there instead of April.

Pulling his jeans on, he rushed shirtless out into the apartment to look for April or a clue as to where or when he was. He saw a coffee cup in the sink and suddenly heard the sound of running water coming from the front guest room.

He rushed there and was about to open the door when he thought better of it and gently rapped on the door. He could hear the water stop and barely heard footsteps coming across the carpeted floor.

When April opened the door wearing a thick terrycloth robe, his breath left his body and he almost could not breathe again.

"Gordon, are you okay?"

He nodded and smiled. He had no idea where he was, but April was there. And that was the only thing that truly mattered.

"Gordon?"

It appeared by April's use of the guest room that it was before their relationship began in earnest, before the trip to Scotland, before everything but high school. But it still didn't matter. She was there with him. He could win her over again as he had so many times.

He wanted to sweep her up in his arms and hold her tightly and smother her with kisses, but he did not. All he could do was stand there speechless with a stupid grin on his face.

"Ah, yes, I wondered if you had made any coffee?"

The irony of his question made him want to laugh, remembering their past conversations about her inability to make coffee.

She said, "Sure" and went into the kitchen where she poured a cup for him. Her horrible coffee had never tasted so good to him.

He felt as if he had been granted a reprieve and while he was usually taciturn in the mornings, he found he could not stop talking. He had no idea what he was prattling on about, but he was almost afraid that if he stopped talking that she would disappear.

April listened to him, but was unable to make much sense of what he was saying, talking one minute about the apartment and the next about going to the Museum of Modern Art. She just nodded her head in agreement. He did not know that she was just as confused by how she had ended up in the guest bedroom's bath, but she still stood and listened because it felt right, as if it were something she was supposed to do.

Her memory was dim as to how she came to be where she was. She could remember being here with Gordon, but it seemed as if she had been somewhere else for a while and then had suddenly just opened her eyes and found herself standing at the sink in the guest bath. She tried to listen closely to what Gordon was saying to give her some clue as to what was going on, but little he said helped her.

"Oh hell, April," Gordon said. "I canna take this any longer," and he dropped the cup into the sink and pulled her against him, kissing her as if he had not kissed her in decades.

April responded to the kiss with equal passion and it was only after a moment or two that they both took a step backward, both surprised and pleased by the kiss.

She looked down at the floor at her bare feet and spoke without meeting his gaze.

"I was starting to wonder what you were waiting on."

Gordon laughed. "My own stupidity, love."

She raised her eyes and met his smile.

"I've been waiting on that kiss since I was sixteen."

"No, really? You never seemed remotely interested in me then. Not that I was anything other than a skinny kid with an accent."

She shook her head, her long curls swinging slightly.

"Why do you think I was always carrying a book with

me when you were over to see Rick? It was my prop in case you might get irritated with me being around."

"A prop? The books were props?" He laughed and it was his turn to shake his head.

"Well, I did read them all, but I felt I had to have something to justify my presence."

He reached past the sink and tentatively touched the soft skin of her hand. She matched his movement and entwined her fingers in his. They both could feel the excitement of desire running through that simple touch.

But the magic of the moment was short lived. Her face clouded over and he recognized the woman from his reality, rather than from this time in Dreamville.

Confusion moved across her features like clouds across a summer field and she looked about the room. He knew that his true April was here now. She began to wobble a bit and then grasped the granite counter to steady herself. This time he saw his April in her eyes and not the April of any other version of Dreamville.

"How, how did we get here, Gordon," she stuttered. "Where were we? I can't remember anything after going into the bedroom to change clothes."

"God, April, you remember Burnock and the

funeral?"

She nodded and looked around the kitchen.

"The apartment looks like it did when we first moved in together."

"I'm not sure when it is, though it is our New York home," he responded.

She glanced at the coffee cups in the sink and smiled forlornly.

"You drank my 'weak-assed' coffee?"

"I would have drunk a pot of it. Where I was before was somewhere I had never been and you weren't there."

She moved close to him and embraced him.

"Hold me then. I don't know where I was. It was just dark and cold. I remember seeing someone, but my brain's a little fuzzy on the details. Hold me. I can't leave you now."

He kissed her forehead and led her into the living room where they could see past the terrace to the bright spring green day beginning to emerge in Central Park below them.

"I don't know how long we'll have here," he said. "I was . . ." and he paused, thinking of the consequences of telling her where he had been. He had never tried to keep anything from her, but his nightmarish future without her made him afraid for her.

"You're keeping something from me, Scotsman," she said touching his cheek. "I've seen that look before."

They sat down on his old green sofa and he brushed a tendril of hair from her face. He did not want to tell her. How many times would he keep hurting her, he asked himself.

"Gordon, don't hide anything from me. I have to know, to be prepared if necessary. Tell me. Could it be worse than what we've already shared in Dreamville? Especially the one version?"

He pulled her onto his lap and she laid her head upon his shoulder. He buried his face in her hair and closed his eyes tightly. He fought it, but he knew he had to tell her.

By the time he had finished his story, she had slid across the sofa, away from him, more confused than ever. Gordon reached to take her hand, but she moved farther away and he stopped to allow her to absorb to news he had related to her.

"Disappeared? Where? We married after the funeral? Why? Gordon, this doesn't make any sense. Are you sure you're remembering everything?"

He sighed in exasperation.

"April, don't you think these are all questions I asked myself? I was there long enough for me to think that I was never going to leave, that I would never see you again. Can you imagine how that felt? How that hurt?"

He walked away from the sofa and stood at the terrace doors, watching the traffic around the park.

"I would have done anything to find you. One minute we were talking and the next minute you were gone and I was over 25 years older. My parents were gone. Most of the staff. I was absolutely alone."

"Gordon, we've always been together in Dreamville. If this was a future Dreamville, where was I? Maybe it wasn't me they found. Maybe I was still alive somewhere. Maybe . . ."

Gordon interrupted her, his voice raised in frustration at what she would not, maybe could not accept.

"For god's sake, April. You were there. You were dead. Buried in the family plot. Why do I have to keep repeating this? What do you want me to say? That it was just something I made up? I wish it were."

April stood and then walked back through their home, toward the guest room without a word to him.

"April, love, don't leave me here," he said and followed her to find her putting her things into her luggage.

"What are you doing? Is this your answer? Leaving me?"

She stopped and realized that she had been so lost in her own train of thought that she had not replied to him.

"Oh god, Gordon, I'm just moving my clothes into our room. You said yourself that we have no idea how long we'll be here. We've spent months in Dreamville. There's no use in being in separate bedrooms."

Gordon leaned back against the door frame in relief. That was when he realized that something was very wrong about their being in Dreamville this time. There was still no sign of Will or Charlotte.

"April, have you seen, ah, well, have you seen them at all?"

She came from the bathroom with her arms loaded with toiletries and stopped.

"No, come to think of it, I haven't seen them since Alex died. But I never saw Will except for those few times. Charlotte, well, I only saw in my shop in Dreamville. Remember? I never saw her at Burnock. Only you and Sheila saw her."

She shifted the things she was carrying and stopped herself from putting them in the valise.

"Why am I packing?" she said and went down the hall with her arms still loaded with shampoo and lotions.

Gordon saw that she was in much worse shape than she was ever going to admit. He followed her and blocked her way from leaving their bedroom.

"You're impeding my progress, Scotsman," she said attempting a smile that never reached her eyes.

"April, stop now. Put those things on the table. Come, lie down next to me on the bed. Let me love you. Love me."

He leaned in and placed his lips against hers. She felt his tenderness as he moved beyond a kiss and began to explore her mouth with his tongue. It felt so familiar and so new at the same time. He lifted her by her hips and carried her to their bed as their kisses became more desperate and deeper.

They spent the rest of the morning making love. Not one tear fell from her eyes, but he could see the pain in her eyes. It was so hard to make love to her when he knew she was so afraid. And he was just as afraid. It was so hard to touch her knowing that he might never touch her again and it was just as difficult not to touch her for the same reason. He shivered thinking of the life he had seen without her.

Later, as they lay together as one in the huge bed, their bodies so close it was almost as if they were one being, their hearts beating together, their breathing in unison.

"Gordon, it seems as if we can't stop bouncing around in time or space or something and the ending is always the same. It's gotten to the point where I sometimes wonder what's real and what's not. Don't you?"

He rolled onto his back and stared at the ceiling, thinking of the ceiling at Burnock. Could they change the future when the excursions into Dreamville were becoming more frequent and more strange?

"Yes. Sometimes. But I always see it in your eyes - when we become synchronized as we are now. I didn't used to see it."

Now it was her turn to be silent and he saw the worry on her face. It frightened him. What did she really think of what he had told her? What she said almost broke his heart.

"Gordon, oh god, how do I say this? Should we leave one another now so that neither of us . . . so that neither of us are hurt or killed?"

Gordon winced. He knew what she was trying to say.

There was a difference between being hurt by heartache and hurt physically. If she were physically hurt . . . no, he could not think of that. It was as if what had happened to them before Burnock were occurring again. He knew what they should do, but it didn't make the pain of it hurt any less.

"If that would save your life, I would drive you to Connecticut now and not look back. I'm not so selfish that I'd hold on to you knowing it might kill you."

She didn't speak and he could feel the few inches between their bodies grow into a gulf that he could not cross.

"The problem is that in the real world we're at Burnock, not here. What good would it do in Dreamville?"

She said nothing in reply and he knew her answer. He had known the answer before, but it was only now that she was seeing the danger. He had thought long before that maybe their separation would put a stop to their traveling in Dreamville. He knew that she was thinking that if the separated that maybe this would become their reality and not Burnock. He got out of the bed and began to dress.

"Well, April, we can try. It might not be too late. We don't even know what Dreamville is. If we're stuck on a true course, then it won't make a difference."

"But, if what we do here can alter life, we have to try if that's what you wanted," he continued.

She hung her head and surreptitiously wiped the tears from her face. She then looked up and him and tried to smile as she nodded her head in agreement.

"Dear, get dressed and get your luggage. We're ending Dreamville now if we can," he said and hurried from the room. He didn't want her to see that this was killing him and he didn't want to see her in pain either.

Two hours later, he sat next to her in the back of his town car while Fred carried her luggage to the front door of her parents' home. They had not spoken since he had left her in the bedroom and he had avoided looking at her as much as possible. It was too hard. He truthfully did not know how to get through this. How could he say good-bye to someone he had loved since he was a teen-ager?

He could not watch her exit the car, but he reached over to her gloved hand and squeezed it.

"If this works, please remember . . ." he had been about to say for her to remember that he would always love her, but he knew that she would never leave the car if he did.

"Remember that life will go on," he said instead and let go of her hand. He felt the air rush in where she had sat and heard the door close. He selfishly wanted to run from the car and stop her, but he did not. He waited quietly while Fred entered the car again and began the drive back to Manhattan.

Within a few minutes of leaving her family home, the thought of going back to their Manhattan home was too much.

"Fred, drive me to La Guardia."

He was going to get on the first plane leaving the airport. Anywhere but there. Anywhere but where she could find him. He had to be strong for her. The thought of the headstone gave him enough reason to protect her.

He saw his life unfolding before his eyes, a life empty, unloved and alone and he frowned. But it would be okay because he knew that somewhere in the world she would be alive and he hoped, happy.

Chapter Three

April's parents asked her few questions about her return home. They could see she was in pain, but they let her grieve in silence the first few weeks after she had returned home. Even her younger brothers gave her space when they came home for spring break.

After a few weeks passed, April felt the need to do something with her time. She started going to work with her mother, where she spent the days constructing quilts that echoed her memories of Scotland, a place that she, at this point in her life's version from Dreamville, had never visited.

Her mother complimented her on the art quilts she was designing and was genuinely surprised by April's ability. She had never thought of April as having any interest in sewing or art. But, then she had never expected her daughter to return home so heartbroken. She wondered if April would ever tell her what had happened to her and Gordon. She believed that they had loved each other as much as any two people could and it was difficult for her to watch April mourn.

April had hoped for the first week that Gordon would come back for her. When he failed to appear, she began to hope for a letter or postcard from him to let her know if he was okay. Finally, when that did not happen, she could take the silence no longer and called his father in a moment of weakness and asked if he had heard from Gordon.

Gordon's father had been kind, but firm. He told her that Gordon had asked that no one be told where he was, especially April. She had apologized for bothering him and for a brief second she heard hesitation in his voice as if he might tell her where Gordon was or might have questions about their break-up himself. But in the end, he failed her as well.

By the time a month had passed and she was still with her parents, she began to believe that she was doomed to live unhappily ever after. She also did not forget the fact that this was exactly what she had been doing when the awful version of Dreamville had taken place. She had been 25 and working with her mother that Christmas season when the nightmare had occurred. She decided that she would go somewhere for the holidays at the end of the year and began to plan some sort of escape plan just in case. She did not want Dreamville or fate or whatever was happening to the two of them to cause the nightmare to come true.

But her 'just in case' plan faded from her mind one day in late spring. She had just completed a quilt of Burnock that her mother was urging her to submit to a local quilt competition. She shrugged it off. The quilt was just one more reminder of what she had lost. She might be able to stop thinking about Gordon consciously, but her subconscious was unrelentingly cruel in putting her love for him in everything she made. She knew when she saw the quilt that she was never going to get over him.

And that, of course, was when her life changed again. She had just begun to give up on Dreamville or reality or the memories of it when it slapped her in the face with a single, sharp pain – the day when Will walked into her mother's quilt shop.

He wasn't wearing the blood stained tennis sweater

she had seen him wearing at Burnock and at first she almost did not recognize him. He was taller than in her memories of him, tanned and blond with an easy manner. Dressed in the typical, but unofficial American prep school manner of khakis and a navy blue blazer, he strolled over to the counter where her mother was inventorying new batiks they had just received.

April breathed in sharply and was backing up towards the rear room where her mother taught classes when she heard her name called by her mother.

"April can help you. April, this gentleman would like to find someone who does quilt restoration. Could you get my book from the shelf in the classroom?"

Moving faster than was necessary, April tried to put as much distance between Will and herself as possible. She was so taken aback by his abrupt appearance that she failed to notice that he had followed her until she had turned from the shelf to find him standing behind her smiling.

She subtly slid around him, smiled slightly and hurried back to the counter where her mother still worked with the bolts of batik cotton.

"April, if you're going to use these batiks, then you're . . . oh, I'm sorry. I didn't see you standing next to April," her mother said to Will.

Will turned to April but showed no sense of recognition of whom she was. April was completely confused. How could he not know her, she thought.

"Is that your work," he asked her, pointing at the quilt she had recently completed that portrayed the highland pasture around the small chapel at Burnock.

She nodded, smiled, left the front counter and went back to her previous position at one of the fabric cutting stations. Instead of staying at the counter where her mother was poring through her book of quilt experts, he followed April through the store.

She sighed and turned to him, ready to tell him to leave her alone when she saw that he truly did not know her.

"Your work is beautiful. Is that from a photograph or your imagination?"

She could not look at him without thinking of the fear she had felt at Burnock, of the disgusting things he had said and done there, but she swallowed her fear and replied as she began to cut shapes in a silvery brown batik.

"Neither."

She could not stand his presence and began to feel

nauseous replying to his questions.

He stared at the quilt for a few minutes and his continued presence began to unnerve her. She was trying to cut the shape of a brook trout from the fabric, but her hands were useless as they shook so much.

"Is that in Maine? It looks a bit like Maine, except for the chapel. Europe, maybe?"

She placed the Gingher scissors down on the table a little louder than she had intended and he turned back to her quickly.

"Neither. Look, I'm sorry. I'm really busy. I'm sure my mother has found someone to do your restoration. If you'll excuse me, now."

He looked down and a small smile tugged at the corners of his mouth.

"Sorry. I really didn't mean to disturb you. It's a beautiful work, though," he said and started to walk away when he stopped.

"How much is it?"

"How much is what?" April said.

He pointed at the Burnock chapel.

"The quilt. How much is it? I'm interested in buying it for my home. It is art, you know. I don't think I've ever seen such a beautiful painting composed of cloth before."

"There are many quilt artists who work in cloth and mixed media. My quilt isn't even close to their work. Maybe you should try one of the galleries in Manhattan."

She began to try to trim the edges of the brook trout again and to ignore him.

He approached the table once more and she saw that he was going to be very difficult to get away from.

"What are you working on now? It looks like you're cutting a small fish. Are you doing a stream scene?"

She put the cloth and scissors back on the table in exasperation. She was actually trying to recreate in cloth a memory she had of walking with Alex along a burn on Gordon's family's property. She remembered the brook trout shadows in the water with branches overhanging the stream and leaves floating on the current of the water.

And her mother was right. She was using mostly batiks to recreate the colors and textures and they were expensive, but she had some money. She would pay her mother for the fabric or work it off. One way or another she would reimburse her for using the expensive cottons. But she had to make the quilts. It was the only way she had of keeping her memories of Burnock alive and as long as she remembered, Gordon would not fade from her thoughts either.

"I really don't want another one. I'd like to buy that one," the man spoke and interrupted her thoughts of Burnock and Gordon.

April had finally had enough. It was not just that she thought of the man she thought had been in Dreamville's influence on her visit to Burnock. It was that he reminded her of every reason she was not with Gordon. She aimed every bit of her loneliness and hatred at him and decided to teach him a very lavish lesson.

"You can't afford it. It's very expensive."

She stared into his eyes, daring him to meet her challenge.

"Well, you might be surprised at what I can afford."

"The quilt is $10,000."

She smiled, believing that she had finally put a stop to his cruel game. She was shocked as he pulled his wallet from his jacket pocket and handed her an American Express card.

"Not a problem. It will be perfect in the foyer of my home."

She realized that her mouth was hanging open and she

quickly snapped it closed as she took the card and slowly walked to the counter where her mother was writing down the name of one of the better quilt restoration experts in the tri-state area.

"What's this for?" her mother asked as April handed her the credit card.

"He just bought my quilt."

Her mother looked at her sadly. She knew what the quilt represented to April. April had poured all her grief and pain over the loss of Gordon into that quilt. She was surprised that April would even part with it. She did not know that it was April's memory of Burnock, but she had been trying to talk April into just showing it for the past few weeks.

"April, you don't have to sell it. I was only griping about the batiks. I know what it means to you."

April shook her head.

"I didn't think he'd take it when I told him the price, but he didn't even blink."

"What do you mean, April?"

"$10,000, mother. $10,000. Now I've got to go get the step ladder to take it down and wrap it up for him. Will you ring it up for me?"

She started away from the counter when her mother grabbed her arm and hissed at her.

"April, you can't be serious. You can't sell that quilt."

"Mother, I can't *not* sell it. In fact, I probably really need to do it. I'm just costing you money here anyway. If he wants to waste his money . . . oh, I don't care. Just ring the damn thing up."

April's mother slid the card through the reader and halfway hoped or expected the card to be rejected. She was unhappy to see the sale go through smoothly.

Across the shop, the man was talking to April as she took the quilt down and began to roll it in muslin. April never said a word to the man, but he would not stop trying to engage her in conversation.

It was at that moment that April's mother wanted to hate Gordon Stewart for whatever he had done to cause her daughter so much pain, so much heartbreak that she couldn't even see the handsome man standing in front of her who not only wanted to talk to her, but maybe even know her more than buying a quilt from her.

Once April had finished wrapping the parcel, she and the man returned to the counter. April was still not smiling, just nodding her head in response to the man's comments.

Her mother handed the man his credit card, receipt, and the information he had originally come into the shop to find.

"Thank you, Mr. Williams. I hope you'll enjoy April's quilt in your home."

"Jonathan. Well, just Jon, actually. I always think of my father when I hear the name Mr. Williams."

April suddenly perked up and interrupted the man.

"Your first name isn't Will?"

He laughed and smiled at her. She had finally responded to his attempts to converse with her.

"No. Jon. Just Jon. May I call you April?"

April nodded, her face showing evident confusion.

He took her hand and shook it, his skin smooth and soft.

"April, it has been a pleasure. You really are more of an artist than you know," he said and walked out the door carrying the wrapped quilt.

Both women watched as he walked down the street.

"I simply cannot wait to tell your father about this. Incredible. April, order all the batiks you want. I think you've found your calling," her mother said and walked back to her office.

April continued to stand at the door and watch Jon Williams walk away with the only tangible evidence she had ever had of her time at Burnock. It was good that both the man and her mother did not remain to see her as the tears slid down her face.

Gordon had never seemed so far away as he did at that moment.

Chapter Four

Another month passed and April had still heard nothing from Gordon. It was as if he had disappeared from the face of the earth and everything that they had gone through were just delusions of Dreamville. By this time she had given up all hope of ever seeing him again. She had almost finished the quilting of the burn quilt and was pleased by how much the scene of the quilt resembled her memory of that spring day walking with Alex. As she examined it, she thought of Alex and realized that in this world he was still alive. Whatever had happened at Burnock in what she had called reality then would not happen because she would never travel there with Gordon.

She smiled and was happy at the thought of Alex still alive when Jon Williams walked back into her mother's shop. She had been running the large free arm quilting machine when he had entered and so when she looked up to see him standing across from her, she almost knocked over an entire rack of cloth bolts at the sight of him. She still had too many frightening memories of what he had said to her at Burnock and this time she was alone in the store with him. Her mother had stepped out to run to the bank and it was still too early for customers.

He was around the quilting machine and helping her to steady herself on her feet before she had the chance to even think.

"You're shaking. I'm really sorry about startling you. I thought you heard me call out your name when I came in."

April put her hands in her jeans pockets to hide their shaking. She tried to remember that this was not Will from Burnock, but instead Jon Williams from New Haven. Unfortunately, his uncanny resemblance to Will and his sudden appearance did little to calm her.

She tried to return his smile and began to straighten up the bolts of fabric she had tumbled into when she had jumped backward.

"I just didn't hear you and I was concentrating on finishing the quilting on this piece. Not your fault."

He leaned in and looked at the burn quilt, touching where she had manipulated the fabrics to make the shadows of the leaves and the brook trout appear on and in the water.

"This is incredible. It's even more beautiful than the one I purchased from you. How do you get the shadows to appear so real?"

She was suddenly embarrassed by his examination of her work and she took a large piece of nearby muslin to cover the quilt.

"It's not finished. I still have quite a bit to do before it's done," she lied, not wanting to have to discuss Burnock with him.

"You know, you really should do a show in Manhattan. I'd even loan my chapel piece for it. Do you have any others?"

She thought of all the ones she had planned from her memories of her short time at Burnock. Everything from the garden to individual landscapes. But she couldn't have enough done for a show for almost a year unless she worked night and day.

"That would be nice, I suppose, but I don't have enough finished pieces for a show and even if I did, I wouldn't even know of a gallery that would be interested," she smiled. She didn't continue. Telling him more would be like saying that selling the quilts would be like selling off pieces of herself. It was almost as if she would be admitting to herself that Gordon was gone from her life forever.

He pulled the muslin away from the quilt and stared at it with the eyes of one who did not so much admire it, but who simply wanted to acquire it. April jerked the muslin back over the quilt and walked away from him.

"What can I help you with today?" she asked lightly as she walked to the front counter.

But he was not going to give up.

"Really, April, I have a friend who has a gallery. She would be very interested in doing a show with your work. I can show her the chapel piece I already have and I know she'll be interested."

"Mr. Williams . . ."

"Jon, please call me Jon. Remember?" he said and grinned, almost trying to cajole her into a better frame of mind. His smile was different from the Will creature and she finally returned his smile with a real one of her own.

"The problem is that I only have two pieces done and you already own one of them. I wouldn't have more work done in time for a show."

"Would you be able to do enough for a show just after Thanksgiving? That would be a perfect time to find buyers."

She shook her head.

"Not by myself. I might be able to do it if I had help with some of the more basic aspects such as the quilting, but the construction and the design I would have to do and I don't know if I could put ten full size quilts together in that time."

He grinned. "Only eight pieces. We can include mine and the one you just finished and I know you've finished it even if you covered it. You made it in a month. With help, you could get the others done by the first of December."

She sighed. It would take so much work. She would have to hire some of her mother's friends to help. On the other hand, she would be so involved in the process of making the quilts that she would have little time to moon over Gordon.

"Jon, you can't put your quilt up for sale."

"That's the beauty of it. We'll hang mine and mark it 'Sold'. That would definitely encourage other buyers. Who knows? You might sell a few or you might sell all of them."

She pursed her lips and frowned.

"Or I might not sell any and your friend would have wasted valuable space when she could be doing a show with known artists."

Jon reached across the counter and touched her hand in enthusiasm. She quickly jerked her hand away and noticed the sharp look in his eyes. Not disappointment. Something else. He was a man who was used to getting his way. She could see that in his eyes and she wasn't sure she liked it. He was so friendly and handsome. Maybe she just had lost her trust in men after Gordon and the events between reality and Dreamville.

"I'm sorry. I startled you again. But I'm just so excited about this. I think it could be a fantastic show."

The cajoling, sweet smile again. April thought that most women would find that smile impossible to resist. Well, what the hell, she thought. If his friend wanted to show her work . . .

"Okay. Show your friend the chapel quilt. If she's really interested, then I can try and put together the others in time for a show. But I should warn you that not all of them will be large works such as the ones you've seen. Some will be smaller wall hangings."

"Like smaller paintings. I don't see a problem in that. If they're as good as the two I've seen, they should be wonderful and I'm sure they'll sell."

"So, deal?" he said and held his hand out to her.

She hesitantly took his offered hand and shook it. His smile was very infectious and for the first time in two months, she found herself laughing.

"Jon, why are you so invested in this? You could end up owning a large quilt that no one likes and find that you overpaid for it. The show could be a huge critical failure. I hadn't even thought of dealing with that aspect of it."

"I don't think so. I think it's going to be a big hit," he said and headed to the door to the store.

"Just wait. You'll see. I have faith in you," and he waved as he walked out.

When her mother returned from the bank, she was surprised, almost stunned to see April smiling for the first time since she had come home.

"April, did you have a good sale while I was gone? Or did something else happen?" She almost said something about Gordon, but caught herself just in time.

April told her mother about Jon's visit and his plan to do a show of her work, of his friend with a gallery in

Manhattan and having a tentative date of the first of December.

"Oh, April. That's so much to do in such a short time. Do you have designs for eight pieces? And do you really feel up to it?"

April grinned.

"Oh, yes, mother. I have dozens in my head. I'll just need help with finishing work. Can I hire some people to help out with that?"

Her mother hesitated. She did not quite know what to say to April.

"Well, I can certainly help and I know a few people we could trust to work, but most of the work is going to be on you. You'll be working night and day. Can you get through that?"

"Oh, mother, for the first time in a long time, I feel as if I could do just about anything. I'm sure I can."

April was so happy and so unburdened by her grief that her mother was almost afraid to ask the one question she had to ask.

"But, April, will they all be of Gordon's home in Scotland?"

April's face fell and she looked at her mother in

surprise. How could her mother know?

Chapter Five

"Scotland? How . . . what makes you think they're of Scotland?"

Her mother walked around the counter and hugged her.

"April, dear, first, I've been to the Stewart home here many times and I've seen pictures of the estate in Scotland. Second, you've been in mourning for months now and all your work looks like the Stewart home in Scotland. I didn't know you'd been there, but the quilts obviously show that you have. Is that when you and Gordon split?"

She pulled away from her mother and walked back to the quilting machine.

"Mother, can we not talk about Gordon? Just be happy for me. And even if the pieces reflect Scotland, does it matter? Just . . . just let me go on with my life. Gordon's gone. The pieces I've done . . ." Her voice trailed off as she walked back to the classroom. Her mother did not see the tears rolling down her cheeks, but once again her mother stood and cursed Gordon Stewart's name under her breath.

April pulled a large sketch pad from one of the classroom shelves, sharpened several colored pencils and sat down at one of the tables to prepare to work on sketches for the quilts and wall hangings. Unfortunately, all she could think of was Gordon and his heather blue eyes. She leaned forward and placed her elbows on the table, only now feeling the dampness on her cheeks.

All she could think of was the last morning she had spent with Gordon and all the nights they had spent together in what they had called their reality. April was no longer thinking of that time as reality and was choosing to think of it as Dreamville instead. Maybe it had never happened. Maybe all the horrible dreams and the nightmares hadn't been real, hadn't been true, just terrified thoughts on her part.

"Hell, maybe I'm the one who's crazy," she said to the empty room and opened the sketch book to begin a drawing of what the next quilt would be. She let her mind wander and let her lose herself in her memories of the few weeks at Burnock, what she saw there, how much she loved it and had loved sharing the time there with Gordon, whether it had been real or not.

She began to focus on the short covered walk from the side of the house into the garden, including the arched grey stone entrance into the beautiful green wonderland of the garden. She thought about it for a moment and the thought crossed her mind of how Judy Garland had opened the door of the black and white Kansas house into the brilliant colors of Oz.

Without realizing what she had done, she had sketched the covered path into the garden, arched open entrance and all, with a simple rose bush laden with lush red blooms overhanging the gravel path beyond the doorway.

She shook her head at what she had drawn. It was exactly the way she remembered first walking into the garden with Alex that cool morning. Now, she thought, the question is how she was supposed to translate that memory into cloth.

She then thought of raw muslin with streaks of

watercolor dyes for the walls and the entrance pieced together much the way the original had been using muslin granite blocks with an oversize keystone at the top of the arch.

The cobbled walk could be composed of muted tan and brown batiks, embellished with small stone chips that would end spread beneath the overhanging rose bush.

I could use green batiks for thick shrubbery, she thought, and thick red satin ribbon roses could be embroidered onto the quilt, giving the passage a dream like quality of moving from a painting into a real place using the flat fabric to move from a one dimensional view to a three dimensional effect with the stones and the large red ribbon roses.

She began to mark the sketch with how she would compose it and then went out into her mother's shop to look for the fabrics she would need. She didn't notice her mother or the other customers in the store. She just went through the aisles, grabbing the bolts of cloth she needed and carrying them back to her sketch.

She cut small swatches from the bolts for each part of the quilt, pinned them to the drawing and wrote above each swatch the fabric type and color lot. She paused for a while thinking of what she could use for the pebbles and thought of the bead shop in Manhattan near 44th Street that sold semi-precious agate chips. Those chips would be perfect for randomly inserting into the cobblestone path before filling the path beneath the rose bush with them.

April shook her head and thought of how long it would take to sew those chips onto the quilt. She saw that this quilt would take more time and cost more simply because of the embellishments she planned. It was also the most ambitious piece she had ever tried.

She stared at the sketch and was saddened by what she had lost. The tears began again and one fat drop splattered on the drawing. She wiped her face with the back of her hand and then tried to use one of the other swatches to dry the paper only to see the wet tear transfer itself to the batik meant for the cobblestone.

Holding the swatch in her hand, she saw that the tear had left a faint stain on the fabric and she knew that somehow she would incorporate that small swatch in the quilt. Her pain physically pulled her into the piece itself. A piece of herself within the quilt piece itself.

That was when she began to become angry. Until now she had yearned for Gordon, mourned his absence, cried for his touch. Now she felt anger growing within her. How dare he? Why didn't he fight for her? He just gave in to her weakness and fear and ended their love affair without giving her the chance to fight to save it, she thought. He had left her alone and broken and hadn't even attempted to see if she were alright.

She threw the pencils across the room and laid her head down on the table, weeping. She knew she could not blame Gordon. They had both agreed that this path was the best. She had been the first to mention it. She just had not known how painful this path would be.

She had no idea that her mother, who was preparing to close for the day, could hear her sobs at the front of the store. Her mother took the cash tray from the register and placed it into the wall safe behind her, the whole time trying not to race back and hold her poor heartbroken daughter. If only April knew how precious children were to their parents, maybe she might understand how ferociously protective her mother felt at that moment.

But this time her mother was not so much angry with Gordon, but with Jon Williams. His little plan to have April do a show of her work was causing April to be even further consumed by the grief she carried inside herself. And somehow, and she knew not how she knew it but she did, Jon Williams was not the handsome and kind man he appeared to be. In fact, for some reason she could not fathom, Jon Williams frightened her more than any man April had ever brought around.

Jon Williams was a bad influence on April and she felt that he wanted something from April. She had to ask herself why he was so insistent that April do this show. It made no sense. Gordon and April had split up for a reason, but she trusted Gordon more than Jon Williams.

At first she was glad to see April talking with another man, possibly leaving her pain behind her. But now she wasn't so sure that Jon Williams was the right person to help April. He might even be dangerous to April, her mother thought as she sat down on the stool at the counter and waited for her daughter's weeping to stop so she could call out to tell her that it was time to close.

Chapter Six

Gordon Stewart was in no better shape than April. He was in actuality, much worse. He had flown to Miami the night he left April on her parents' doorstep and had spent the last two months walking the streets of Cocoanut Grove, watching the constant parade of locals, tourists, con artists, and lovers while trying to keep from drowning himself in scotch.

He had had no idea of just how painful being without April would be. He was constantly on the watch for either Will or Charlotte, yet never saw them. He could not understand it nor could he understand why he and April had not returned to the reality of Burnock. Like April, he was also beginning to believe that their time at Burnock was Dreamville and that this sorry sad mess of a life was actually his reality.

His parents had remained in contact with him and had promised to relay any information about April if she might be in trouble. They asked if he were taking his medications and he had laughed and lied. He hadn't had anything since Burnock when he realized that he was not ill.

No, he had had no medication except for the expensive scotch with which he tried to numb his senses.

He had rented a small house near the grove that was furnished with some rather fine local antiques and a small separate building that housed a lap pool. The place had a nice garden and a gardener he rarely saw, but then he rarely went into the garden and only swam laps in the morning to try and wash away the effects of the previous night's bottle of scotch.

If he had known that Will or someone who appeared to look like Will was subtly wooing April with promises of an art show in Manhattan and unending flattery, he would have made his way back to Connecticut in a heartbeat. But he could not know because his parents did not know and therefore could not tell him.

Each morning he woke to feel as if sharp knives were being stabbed into both his head and heart. Part of it was the scotch, but most of it was the almost unendurable pain of missing April.

Not that women had not tried to gather his attention and the more brazen actually attempted seduction. They did and often with no success. He could not imagine ever loving a woman other than April. Perhaps it was a combination of his sad, unapproachable manner or the pain that lingered in his blue eyes that made some women seem to think they could help. Whatever it was, he never succumbed to their offers. He would smile, sometime wave, but he would always walk away from them, usually ending up alone at the movie theater midway down the main street of the Grove, pulling a small flask from his pocket in the dark and filling the empty soda cup that he had dumped the soda from. The ushers at the theaters knew of his habit, but never spoke to him of it. He never bothered anyone and he always paid for the soda even when he didn't drink it. The generous tips he gave them never hurt either, and only encouraged their silence.

After two months of just going through the motions of life, he awoke one morning and instead of swimming, instead went through the house gathering every bottle of liquor he could find and tossing them into a can that he threw into the outside trash bin. He woke that morning knowing that he couldn't go back to April and that he also couldn't waste his life drinking alone in the Grove.

He began to do the things that he had been doing before April had entered his life again. He began to pay attention to his work again and thought of Rick. It had been about this time that he had hired Rick to work for him and he realized that he needed Rick but was not sure if Rick would want to work with him.

That afternoon Gordon took the chance of calling Rick's home and thankfully Lisa did not answer. At first Rick had been extremely cold to him. He understood that. He couldn't imagine the pain that he might have caused April. But after talking with Rick for a while, he finally got Rick to consider coming to work for him and tried to extract from him a promise not to tell April anything.

"That won't be hard," Rick had said. "You're the last person I want to mention to her. You've caused enough pain for everyone as it is."

Gordon was surprised by his bluntness. He had expected Rick to be cool, but had never expected such blunt honesty.

"Is she okay, Rick?"

"What does it matter to you, Gordon? Listen, I'll think about the job. But I'm not going to lie to her. If I take the job, I'm going to tell her, though I don't think she'll have much to say about you. She hasn't spoken about you since you dumped her on the sidewalk at our parents' house."

Gordon started to defend himself and then stopped. What good would it do? Rick would never understand about Dreamville. Hell, he could barely understand it. He finished the phone call with a promise from Rick to call him back before the end of the week and let him know his response to Gordon's job offer.

He thanked Rick and sat on the stranger's sofa and looked around the room. It was time to go home, whether April was there or not. He couldn't hide out in Florida any longer. If he stayed there one more day, it would be a day too long.

That night he found himself on a flight to New York and landed at La Guardia at midnight. He had arranged for Fred to meet him at the airport and was back at his New York home an hour later. The place was cold and empty as his footsteps echoed against the marble floors of the foyer. He went to the kitchen to find that Frank had made arrangements for the cupboards and refrigerator to be fully stocked.

He grabbed a club soda from the refrigerator and drank most of the liquid from the small bottle in just a few gulps. With all his might, he resisted picking up the phone and calling April. How was he going to live here without her? And he realized that perhaps he never really had lived with her, except in the delusion produced by the place they both had called Dreamville.

He went to his bedroom and stared at the large bed and remembered the time in the real world when he had driven April away the first time. He had laid down upon the bed and believed that she was gone forever. He had underestimated her tenacity.

So why had she allowed him to drive her away again and not search for him? His April, his real April, his love, never gave up or gave in. Then he realized that he was being unfair in always expecting her to fight for him while he continually pushed her away. Maybe she wanted him to fight for her for a change or maybe she wanted nothing more to do with someone who kept forcing her away.

He wanted a drink badly at that moment, but decided to shower and get some sleep before trying to work tomorrow. He knew that his scotch habit was becoming a little too convenient. And he would have stayed away from it had he not found one small item April had forgotten in the shower – a bottle of her lavender scented shampoo. When he walked into the bathroom, he could smell the faint scent of the shampoo and for a brief second he thought she might be there and then knew she was not.

That was all it took to break his will. He walked back to the kitchen and grabbed a bottle of scotch from the cabinet and poured a generous glass that he quickly drank. He felt the fire of the liquor coursing through him and poured another glass that he carried back to the bedroom. He undressed, drank the second glass and succumbed to sleep, never even thinking that his life would be any different in the morning than it was now.

The bright sunlight and the noise of New York woke him the next morning. He rubbed his temples trying to ease the hangover headache that was just beginning to bloom inside his head. He ran to the bathroom and thought for a moment that he might be sick, but instead entered the shower, turned on the water and steam, and sat on the marble shelf.

"Well, I've found myself in this position before," he said aloud, thinking of the last time he had made love to

April there and the time he had tried to make her leave only to be followed to Scotland by her unrelenting stubbornness. He shook his head and could see why she had not followed him this time. This time he had gone too far.

Why couldn't she understand that he was trying to protect her? But then he really couldn't understand it himself. It was to protect them not just from the dire predictions of Dreamville but also from the shades of Will and Charlotte. He simply could not understand why she did not understand that he was doing this for her. He believed himself cursed and he could not bear for her to become the victim of that curse.

After he finally had dressed and had coffee, his mobile rang and he saw Rick's name appear on the iPhone. He hoped that Rick had some good news for him. At least to tell him that he would take the position working for Gordon and a small part of him wanted Rick to just say that April was okay, but Gordon doubted Rick would do that.

"Rick, how are you this morning? I'm back in Manhattan now and ready to get back to work. Have you made a decision?"

He could hear a sharp intake of breath on the other end of the call and he feared that Rick was about to decline his offer.

"Gordon, I've talked it over with Lisa and I've decided that I'll take the position with your firm. Your terms were generous and as long as I'm not cleaning up messes I didn't make and everything is legit, I think it can work out."

Rick was unpleasant, as if he were doing Gordon a favor, not the way someone would inquire about a potential job.

Gordon almost told him to forget it at that moment. The last thing he needed was to have to deal with April's angry brother on a daily basis. But then Rick surprised him with his next statement.

"I've also talked to April about it. I wouldn't and won't hurt her anymore than she's been hurt, but she encouraged me to take the job. She's found something for herself now and seems to be moving on."

When Gordon didn't respond to that bit of information, Rick immediately felt remorse for saying it. Something told him that Gordon wasn't any happier with the separation from April than she was. A small part of Rick had wanted to hurt Gordon and now that he saw he had, he regretted it.

"Well, that's good then. Can you start Monday? I've let a lot of things slide in the past few months and I know there's a great deal of paperwork waiting for me at the office."

"Sure, Gordon. Monday's fine. I'll see you then."

As Rick was starting to click off his cell phone, he was surprised to hear Gordon's voice again.

"Rick, is she okay? I know I have no right to ask, but . . . I just want to know she's okay. I do worry about her. I know you may not believe that, but I do."

Rick sighed and truly felt sorry for Gordon. He and Lisa had spent so much time with Gordon and April that he was stunned when Gordon broke off their relationship without any reason. Certainly not a reason that April would give.

"April's is doing okay. I'm going to be very honest with you. It was brutal. I didn't think she would ever come out of it and I wanted to hate you for hurting her, but somehow I thought or hoped that perhaps you were missing her just as much."

"I have missed her. I do, Rick, but . . . the whole thing is too complicated."

"Gordon, I'm going to work with you and we'll have a very professional relationship, but I can't be your friend and listen to stories about your personal life or how you hurt when I know how much she hurts. She's my sister. She comes first. I'm sorry, Gordon, but that's how it has to be."

Gordon ran his hand through his hair and nodded.

"Yes, Rick. I understand. But, just one thing - if she's ever in danger, will you please tell me? I won't say anything about the situation otherwise. Just promise to let me know if she's in trouble. Okay?"

"Okay, Gordon. I've got to go now. See you Monday morning at your office. And thank you for the position. Thank you," Rick said and clicked off his cell phone.

Gordon sat his mobile down on the granite countertop and looked at it, wanting to pick it up and call April, but he wouldn't be that selfish. From the conversation with Rick, he had gathered that it might have been much more difficult for April than for him and that it would only be cruel to call her. At least she knew where he was now and Rick, whether he realized it or not, would be their only true connection.

He felt the back of his hair against the collar of his

white shirt and decided to head downtown to get his hair cut. He was surprised that he hadn't grown a full beard to go with the longer hair in his state of oblivion to his own needs. He saw now that the scotch had been more than a little too successful at numbing his pain. He certainly had to clean himself up before seeing his parents.

And that, in itself, was another problem for him. He could not go to their home in Connecticut. It would be too dangerous for him to possibly run into April or see her on the street, not to mention the temptation of walking to her house just to catch a glimpse of her the way he had in high school.

He called his father and let him know that he was back in Manhattan and tried to set up a time for having supper together in the city. He knew his mother would want him to come there, but she would have to understand that that was not a possibility.

His father was glad to hear his voice and agreed that supper in the city would be a better choice than Gordon coming to Connecticut. Gordon told his father he would call them at home tonight and they could work out where and when they would dine then.

Chapter Seven

April's mother was astonished by the quilts that April was designing and constructing. As much as she hated to admit it, Jon Williams was right – they were paintings composed of cloth, thread, and semi-precious stones. The Arch quilt was breathtaking, not just in the design, but in the smallest details that April had added to it as she worked on it. The old fashioned roses made of silk red ribbon were embellished with tiny garnet beads that from a distance looked like dewdrops weighing the blossoms down toward the agate gravel path.

April had moved on to other quilts and wall hangings and the classroom was full of women doing the basic quilting, creating backings, sewing sleeves for hanging the pieces, and creating bias strips or fabric shapes when needed.

The quilts had energized everyone. The women who frequented her mother's shop and those who assisted in the completion of the pieces were inspired by April's designs. This, in turn, brought new customers and more business into her mother's store. Where she had had a small clientele previously, she now had a steady stream of new customers and new students for her classes.

April had been in the process of piecing one of her quilts when she approached her mother at the cash register to see if she had received the delicate silk embroidery thread for one particular quilt. Her mother was in a lively conversation with one of their new customers and April started to turn away when her mother called her over.

"Dear, I wanted you to see this beautiful embroidery work. The blackwork is beautiful."

April looked down and saw nothing but what looked like vertical and horizontal lines of thread that almost formed a chart. April stared at it and something about it made her think of Dreamville.

"Here, April, you're looking at it upside down. It's a blackwork chart of her complete ancestry and descendants."

"Genealogy chart, in other words," the customer said and laughed. "A big family when you include the grandchildren."

April turned the piece of cloth back to its former position and she saw something she had never thought much of – Gordon's discussion at Burnock of dimensions and space and how people used to believe there were only three dimensions and that accepting time as a fourth had been unheard of.

But in this simple piece of blackwork detailing the woman's family, she could see more than just the dimensions Gordon had discussed. She saw how that everything was interconnected, how even the simplest choice could have implications on how reality could be seen.

"It really is incredible," April said to the customer, excused herself and rushed back to the small corner where she kept her sketch book. She took a large blank sheet of paper and began drawing the various interpolations of Dreamville that she and Gordon had experienced.

Sometimes the lines actually went off in directions that had no end and sometimes they moved back to earlier events and went in different directions. By the time she had finished the chart, she could count at least 10 variations forward and countless variations that could be extrapolated from those ten.

Dreamville, according to the sheet she had filled with her scribbles was endless. She leaned back in the chair and needed Gordon now more than she ever had. He had been right about Dreamville and while she was excited about what she had discovered, she was also terrified at the implications it presented. One wrong move. One simple choice and she could be with Gordon forever and she could never have had him in her life at all. The complications were dizzyingly endless.

But the largest question remained – how had she and Gordon become so involved in these different futures and pasts they called Dreamville? And how did Will and Charlotte seemingly move effortlessly between the realities? In other words, how did she and Gordon stop the shifts and stay in one reality? Could they stop dreaming? Which of the lines would put them on the place that stopped the dreaming? Which reality was their true reality?

She was chewing on the pencil when her mother came back to the classroom where she had sat up her own small table she had been using for sketching.

"April, are you okay? Your face lost all color when you looked at that genealogy chart. Does it have to do with being separated from Gordon?"

April quickly closed her sketch book and embraced her mother. For some stupid, pointless reason, she felt as if she had discovered something important. She wasn't a physicist, but she knew that her lines on that sketch meant something and for the first time she felt good about what Dreamville could be to her and Gordon.

"I'm fine, Mom. Overwhelmed, maybe, but otherwise fine."

She looked around the room and saw all the women helping her construct a view of Burnock that she had seen and yet had in some aspects only imagined. She shook her head as if to shake off the confusion the chart had caused and tried to return herself to what she had to do now.

She still felt that her pieces were nothing special compared to the real art quilts she had seen, but her mother had continuously told her otherwise. Now she looked at the quilts being completed and thought that she might be wrong about what they really were. Maybe the quilts were clues to her true reality. Maybe her work was just as good, and in some instances as her mother pointed out more inspired than other art quilts that she had seen, but that was not what the quilts were. Maybe they were something much more valuable. Maybe they were hope.

Maybe the quilts were just like the chart - a map back to her home, her real home with Gordon. She thought of the early mapmakers and how their maps were now considered works of art, but they had actually been visual representations of the known world then.

Maybe her quilts were like that, but instead representations of worlds yet unknown.

Chapter Eight

News of what April was doing had spread through the small community and even the local newspaper did an article on April's return and her art. It was discomfiting to April. She had only started working with her mother to bury her pain and to hide. Instead, it had the opposite effect. She had become well known in her small community. Enough so that the high school had brought their art classes and home economics classes to see what April was designing, to show the teenagers that art knew no boundaries or methods and that something as basic as sewing could become art. The students were fascinated by the depth in the pieces, from the shadows of the fish in The Burn to the dimensional movement of the viewer through The Arch.

When they saw great size of The Chapel and the mist that hung in the Highlands, they were surprised that such a single large quilt could be made and they felt the sadness inherent in the stones and monuments in the plot next to the Chapel.

The Thistle was the one that everyone who saw it wanted to touch. Somehow, April had actually made it look as if she had actually sewn a live thistle into the background fabric, with needled stems and leaves, and topped with the silky pinkish purple blossom. April spoke little of their construction. She was too busy to speak with the visitors, but she offered them all friendly smiles and turned their questions to her mother or the women helping her.

The strangest of all the quilts was actually one that seemed the simplest but was deceptively ornate. It was called The Yellow Room. It was a simple wall with a mullioned window that was partially open with a translucent and gauzy floor length curtain that seem to be blowing in a non-existent wind. The walls appeared to be covered with some sort of yellow floral wallpaper, but each tiny flower was embellished with French knots topped with citrine gemstone chips. Beyond the window and the billowing curtain were the same blue green Highlands from

The Chapel quilt, but they were blurred as if seen through glass and cloth. The only odd item was in the lower right corner where the beginning of a length of dark wood disappeared from view.

Only April knew that the disappearing wood was the door into Gordon's bedroom. It was when she first sketched that wood that she realized that she would never lose her memories or her love for Gordon and Burnock.

By the first of November, almost all ten pieces were nearing completion or completed. Jon Williams came several times a week to survey her progress and had earlier brought Nora Epstein, the gallery owner, with him in August to reassure her of April's progress. The woman had told April then that she was very impressed with the work and thought that the show would be very successful.

"Have you thought of a name for your show?" she had asked April.

Before April could respond, Jon interrupted her and said that he thought "Highland Dreams" would be good. April looked at Jon Williams's face and felt unsettled as he blithely threw out the word "Dreams" as part of the title. But she had no time to react to his suggestion. The Nora woman had wrinkled her nose at it.

"Hmm, I don't know. That sounds like a romance novel and there is nothing romantic about these works. They're almost haunting in their theme. Surely, April, you have an idea."

April shrugged her shoulders. The pieces may have had a haunted look to them, but they were all built on her great love for Gordon so how could they not be romantic, she wondered.

It was her mother who saved her from both Nora and Jon. Her mother had been eavesdropping on the conversation since she had decided she did not care for Jon Williams. She felt he was stupid if he did not see that every part of every piece was a piece of April and her love for someone Williams did not know.

"What about "Pieces of April?" she asked. "There was a beautiful song I remember hearing ages ago called *Pieces of April*. It seems to make sense since the quilts are pieces April created."

The Nora woman smiled broadly. "Brilliant! It goes beyond the art of the quilts and actually embraces the parts that make up each piece. Absolutely! Pieces of April is what we'll call the show."

Jon Williams tried to smile, but April's mother could

see a tightness around his eyes that said to her that he once again did not like not getting his way. But before he could veto the title of the show, April spoke up.

"Sounds fine to me. I suppose you need the names of each work for the catalog?"

"Yes," Nora said and walked back to the classroom with April, leaving Jon Williams and April's mother standing over The Thistle.

He lifted up one corner of the quilt and dropped it as if it were poisoned. She saw for the first time that Williams not only disliked April's work, but also, perhaps, April. When he realized he had allowed her to see a small part of his true self, he smiled broadly and hugged her shoulder.

"Nora, of course, is correct. It is a brilliant title," he said and walked back to where Nora and April were standing.

April's mother stepped backward away from Williams, His touch on her shoulder had felt, well, wrong was the only word she could think of. So wrong. She wanted to wash her bare shoulder where Williams had touched her. It was as if she had been touched by some negative, evil force. She was trying to think of a time when Williams had ever touched any of them, but before she could continue with the thought, she was approached by a customer and the thought slipped away from her mind.

In the classroom, April was showing Nora the sketches of the eight new works, besides The Chapel and The Burn, which she had previously seen.

"The pieces are The Chapel, The Burn, The Arch, The Thistle, The Yellow Room, The Bench, The Auld Moon, The Trestle Table, The Sea, and The Claw Foot Tub," she said to Nora who was hastily scribbling the names to prepare for the catalog.

"We'll have the catalog completed except for the final pictures by mid-November. I'd like to include your sketches in the catalog with the photographs of the finished pieces. Sort of an artistic process thing, you know."

"But by then, we'll have to have the professional photographs of each piece. Do you want to describe them or say anything about the inspiration for each one in the catalog?"

April shook her head.

"No. The pieces should speak for themselves. Truthfully, I feel a bit pretentious about even having a show for them. I mean, they're special to me, but I can't see that they would be for anyone else. I'm really afraid you're going to lose money on this."

Nora laughed and embraced April.

"Oh, Jon, you were right about her. She still doesn't know how good they are."

She turned to April and grinned.

"April, if I could get ten more from you before the show, I would. I know they're going to be a great success. Just wait and see. You'll be surprised by not just the money you make, but by the attention you'll receive for them."

April smiled slightly and excused herself from them to go and help one of the women working on The Bench quilt to get the bias binding angled the way she wanted so that it created shadows next to the shrubbery. She disliked talking about the quilts, especially as art. Sometimes they were more like geometry problems to be solved – matching corners, manipulating the fabric to fit into the angles and circles she needs. Even the asymmetrical pieces had to be precisely placed. She had discovered when she first began The Chapel that quilt making was far from simple work for housewives. Probably some arrogant man had thought of that epithet, she had thought. Even the precise length of the stitches had to be perfect. But she still could not imagine that anyone would come to the show, much less purchase one of them.

April had no idea that Gordon's family had been carefully tracking her progress, especially with the sudden announcement of the show. They were astounded to see their garden at Burnock as one of April's pieces in a photograph in the local paper. They discussed with one another how she had such an intimate knowledge of their home in Scotland. In this world, April had never been there and they knew nothing of Dreamville or her possible future there.

They debated over telling Gordon about the gallery show in December, but were spared that task when he called them instead, having seen a one sheet mailer in Rick's briefcase shortly before Thanksgiving.

"Why didn't you tell me what she was doing?" he asked them angrily.

"Gordon, you broke things off with the poor girl and yet you still want us to spy on her for you. Well, I won't do it anymore," his mother said.

"Claire, I don't think that's what he's asking," Gordon's father said on the extension phone.

Gordon paused and then apologized to both of them.

"I'm sorry. You're absolutely right. I've just been worried about her. I'm glad that she's found something fulfilling," he said.

"I don't think any of this would have happened if that Williams man hadn't seen her work," his mother said.

Gordon felt an electric shock run through his body and almost dropped the phone.

"What Williams man? Who is he? Where is he from?"

"I don't know, Gordon. There was very little about him in the newspaper. Most of the article centered on her Scottish themed pieces. Which reminds me, did you two go to Burnock? She has captured it in incredible detail," his mother continued.

"Mother, this Williams man. Have you or father seen him? Does he live nearby?"

His mother sighed loudly in exasperation.

"Gordon, we know nothing about him. If it bothers you so much, check into it. As for the show, we've bought tickets and will be going. Since it's our home in those pieces, I'm interested in seeing them close up."

"Of course, I could go over to the Norris's shop, but I would feel rather uncomfortable doing that. And there's no reason to make things difficult for April right now," she said and then quickly broke off her speech.

Gordon stared out the window of his office at the Manhattan skyline. He wasn't thinking about the show. He was thinking that Will was probably this Williams man and he wondered how April could not see it.

"Would you mind buying a third ticket? I'd like to attend as well," he said.

"Gordon, do you think that's wise?" his father asked. "Things have been complicated enough as it is. There are many changes you've not known about."

What he did not tell Gordon was that he often talked with April's father over the past eight months and that the situation was truly more complicated than Gordon could possibly know.

"Yes, I know it's been a rough year. I've had to live through it as well. But the show is next Tuesday and I am going. I think April and I can both be mature enough to see one another without any great drama."

"But, Gordon, there's . . ." his father started to say when Gordon interrupted him.

"Buy the ticket and meet me at my place or I'll buy one myself and see you there. Either way, I'm going. Now, I've got things to take care of here before the weekend begins. I'll talk to you later," he said and hung up the phone.

At his parents' home, his mother walked into his father's study and stood there confused.

"What are we going to do? We should have told him. My god, he'll be devastated. This Williams man has become so close to April," she said and collapsed into one of the leather chairs opposite the desk.

"Claire, he did it to himself. He'll have to be a man and deal with it now. We've done all we can do."

Gordon's father leaned back in his chair and swiveled around to look out the window at the distant white clapboard house that April and her family lived in. God, help Gordon, he thought. He's going to need it.

Chapter Nine

The day of the show left April exhausted and her back ached from being on her feet for most of the day. The pieces were all gone now and she was home dressing for the trip into the city. Her entire family was insistent on going, although she kept telling them that it would be fine and that she wasn't going to be disappointed if the show was received poorly. She was just glad that the work and anticipation were almost over. She felt that after tonight she could finally rest.

She slipped into a coral sheath and her mother came into her bedroom asking if she needed any help getting ready.

"Mother, I'm fine."

She paused and turned to her mother.

"Gordon's parents are going to be there, aren't they?"

Her mother nodded and came over to where April sat. She took April's long hair into her hand and began to twist her curls upward into a smooth French twist.

"Something special for tonight, don't you think?"

April smiled in the mirror at her mother's reflection.

"Yes, I suppose so. I'm supposed to be a grown-up now, aren't I?"

Her mother finished with April's hair and leaned down to kiss her daughter's cheek.

"Perhaps, but you'll always be my little girl."

As her mother left the room, April glanced at her own reflection in the mirror and saw that she wasn't just a young girl now. She was an adult in more ways than one and she had survived the past eight months without Gordon. As she stood to leave to join her family, she felt a quick twinge at the base of her spine.

Even if the show were a success, she was definitely going to give herself a break. She had worked too hard and her body was telling her so.

By the time the Norris family arrived at the gallery, Rick was standing outside the building with an umbrella, waiting for his sister's arrival. He was as nervous as he could be about this whole evening. He had only found out today that Gordon was going to be at the show and he had pleaded with Gordon to leave April alone, to let her have her peace, but Gordon refused.

Gordon still had not arrived by the time April and the rest of his family arrived and Rick hoped desperately that Gordon had changed his mind. It was bad enough that Gordon's parents were already there, but then they were there to see April's rendition of their home as much as anything.

April's father helped her from the limousine and she looked up in awe at the sign above the gallery that said in cream letters against a pale lavender background:

PIECES of APRIL – The Art of April Norris

It was odd to see her name there as if she were someone important. She laughed and shook her head. She thought of the Shakespeare play *Much Ado About Nothing* and laughed a little harder just as her back began to ache again.

Rick led her into the gallery that was packed with people. Lisa was waiting by the door and hugged her and handed her a club soda.

"Are you ready? It's a full house. And here comes Nora and that Williams man."

Lisa and the rest of the Norris family felt the same about Williams as April's mother did, but they said nothing about it to April. He had made this evening possible for her. They had to give him that, albeit begrudgingly so.

Nora leaned in to air kiss April's cheeks and took her by the elbow to lead her through the room to introduce her to various potential buyers. Before they stepped into the crowd, April stopped to thank Jon Williams for his help and started to offer him her hand, but he stepped back and gave her a short bow and a large smile.

"My pleasure, dear April. Anything for you."

As they moved through the parting crowd of people who recognized April from her picture on the back of the catalog, Nora murmured that she wanted April to greet the big buyers first. April looked at the prices on the pieces on the walls and was stunned. When she had sold The Chapel to Jon Williams for $10,000 so many months ago, she would never have believed that the other pieces would have even higher prices on them. The price on The Arch stunned her. It said $75,000 and it had a red dot next to the price.

"Nora, I think someone made a typo on the price on The Arch. I think there's one zero too many and there's a dot next to it."

Nora smiled and her laughter tinkled like the sound of the champagne glasses around the room.

"No mistake, April," she whispered. "That's the price and the dot means that it's already been purchased. We had one buyer who insisted on seeing the show earlier today. He went straight to The Arch and said he wanted it. Paid for it immediately as well."

April stopped and stared and Nora and Jon Williams. "Jon, you didn't . . ."

He shook his head.

"I wish I had, but someone else beat me to it. In fact, I think they're making their way here now," he replied and turned.

Gordon had seen Will first and was making his way to where Will stood next to April. Even with her hair in the French Twist he recognized the back of her long neck. He was pushing people aside roughly trying to get her away from Will when April turned to face him.

It was the moment that both families had dreaded

more than any other moment of the evening. Even April and Gordon were unprepared for what was about to happen.

April turned and time seemed to slow down as she saw him and Gordon saw her beautiful face first and then looked down to see that she was not only pregnant, but largely pregnant, almost ready to give birth at any moment.

He stopped and the champagne glass slipped from his hand, shattering upon the concrete floor of the gallery. He started to speak and found his trembling voice was almost gone as Will began to laugh loudly.

"This is what you missed, Stewart. You should never have left her. It was just what I was waiting for. I was going to have her finally. And then I found out about this and I couldn't take her with that," Will said and pointed at April's belly.

At that moment April looked up and saw Will and not Jon Williams and she was about to scream when she felt as if someone had spilled water all over her dress and the water flowed down her dress and onto the floor. Suddenly the backache she'd been enduring all evening turned into an agonizingly long pain and she looked at Gordon and started to cry. She understood then that the backaches had been the precursors of labor and that Jon Williams had kept her so distracted that she had thought only of her work and not the pregnancy, not Gordon's child conceived the last time they had been together before he left her at her parents' home.

She reached out to Gordon's hand in desperation. He had to see what was happening, she thought.

"Gordon, our baby's coming. Nora, I'm sorry I've made a mess of things." For the first time in the months since Gordon had dropped her at her parents did she remember the missing piece of the puzzle of her life. She was very pregnant and the baby was coming now.

Will vanished as if he had never been there. Strangely enough, no one even mentioned him after he disappeared. The crowd around April and Gordon moved away as Gordon went to hold April in his arms. For the first time in almost a year, his life felt right again. He called out for help and April's younger twin brothers both appeared to assist him in leading April from the gallery.

April was unaware of the tears falling from her eyes or that she was crying aloud in pain from the labor. She wrapped her arms around Gordon and passed out. She had lost the will to fight. Only the wait for this moment had kept her going. Only this moment had kept her alive.

Chapter Ten

The chaos that had ensued with the departure of the Norris and Stewart families was meaningless to Nora. She had a show to finish and she had her staff surreptiously clean up after April left while she continued to talk with art critics and buyers. She was in her milieu and she was ecstatic. April's labor could not have come at a better time for her show. Buyers who always pretended to be blasé and bored were always excited by any drama at a show and *Pieces of April* was truly a great drama as Nora made sure the ill fated lovers' story was circulated through the room. While April was being rushed to New York Presbyterian, each of her art pieces was being sold as well as being critically praised by the art community in general.

In the limousine, April awakened and began

apologizing to Gordon for not calling him and he began apologizing for leaving her alone.

Finally, her father, whose nerves were wracked by the events at the gallery turned to them from the front seat.

"Enough 'I'm sorry' from both of you. April, hold on, we're almost there. Stew, did Claire get a ride with Rick and Lisa?" he asked from his seat next to the driver.

Gordon's father who was in the back of the limousine with April and Gordon nodded and tried to ease April's labor pains as best as he could. It had been a long time since he had delivered a baby and he had no desire to deliver his own grandchild.

"April, try to take deep breaths and relax your body. We'll be at the hospital in just a few minutes. Just hold on," he said.

And that's exactly what she did. She held onto Gordon's hands as if he would disappear at any moment. What the rest of the family did not know was that both she and Gordon were afraid that they or one of them would disappear with the whims of Dreamville. What April did not know was that Gordon was horribly afraid that Will had done something to hurt her and the baby. He knew Will would do anything to cause him to lose them. He

111

could not help but think of the headstone in the family plot that was dated exactly a month from today. Would they marry sometime in the next month and then would he lose her forever, he asked himself.

While April held onto him and he tried to calm her breathing, they finally arrived at the hospital. Gordon's father had called ahead and had made sure the obstetrical unit was prepared for their arrival.

As Gordon lifted her from the back of the limousine to the wheelchair, he held on to her hands as the orderlies pushed her through the halls of the hospital. He did not notice their families falling back into the waiting room or that two women were shoving a surgical robe and hat onto him or that they were scrubbing his hands and then pushing him down onto a stool next to the bed where April had been undressed and changed into a hospital gown, her legs up in air and her paper shod feet shoved into stirrups.

What he did see was that she was in a great deal of pain and that there was blood on the floor between her legs.

"April, love, hold on. I love you. I will never leave you again."

And those were the key words that were waiting to be

said for the two of them to be transported back to their reality in Scotland.

April screamed from a labor pain during the transition and it took a few seconds before Gordon saw that they were no longer at the hospital, but in the yellow bedroom. She was wearing one of his old t-shirts and the bed was covered in blood the way the floor of the hospital's labor suite had been.

This time they had not only been transported, but their child was arriving as the transition took place. Instead of a room full of doctors and nurses, all professionally trained for any emergency, there was just April, him and their baby making its way into the world.

"Fuck no!" April screamed, seeing what had occurred, yet she had to begin to push their child into the world. She could feel the baby moving down and the instinctive need to push overwhelmed all other thoughts.

Gordon instinctively went to stand at the foot of the bed between her legs. He could see the matted thick black hair of their child's head as it emerged from the birth canal. He guided the child's head with his hands and then gently moved the baby's body from his wife and onto the quilt beneath her. The baby was breathing and looking at him with what seemed to be wide open eyes that were too wise for his age.

Shouldn't there be crying? He leaned down to the baby and could feel the breath of his child upon his cheek.

Things began rolling over in Gordon's mind. He needed to do certain things. He ripped the bottom of his own shirt and tied off the cord before he cut it with his pocket knife. He rushed the baby to the bathroom and wrapped it in a large white bath sheet he pulled from the linen press. He was still concerned that the baby was not crying, but the child was staring at him with eyes that were those of a completely self aware individual. The child was still breathing with healthy pink skin and it grasped Gordon's pinky finger as he rushed back to where April still lay upon the bed.

Gordon remembered that there was something very important that he had to do to help April and he placed the baby in a crib that was waiting near the bed. He didn't think about how the crib got there, he just thanked God that it was.

"April, you still have a little more work to do. I think you have to deliver the afterbirth or you'll get very ill. Can you push just a little more for me? I promise that it won't be much more."

Her face was covered in sweat and her braided hair had come loose and the curls were plastered against her face. Half sitting, she nodded, but then pointed her head in the direction of the crib.

Gordon smiled.

"The baby's fine. It seems quiet for a newborn, but then I don't really know how newborns are supposed to sound."

April sat up again and pushed once more, this time expelling the afterbirth from her body. Gordon ran to the bathroom again and returned with armfuls of towels and linens. April had laid back on the bed, but her legs were still bent at the knees and she looked exhausted and paler than usual.

Gordon began to wash the lower half of her body carefully. It appeared that the bleeding had subsided once she had delivered the afterbirth, but the pallor of her face concerned him. He watched as she closed her eyes and her head sank into the pillow.

"April! April, wake up! Don't sleep yet," he yelled and she opened her eyes quickly and looked around the room.

"Is something wrong? Where is the baby, Gordon?

Bring the baby to me." Her voice was hoarse as she tried to speak. She had been unaware of how loud she had been screaming during the birth.

He exhaled in relief that she seemed to be regaining her color and grabbed the dirty linens and just tossed them into the bathroom. He stepped softly over to the crib where the baby looked up at him as if it was simply waiting quietly for its parents to finish their tasks. Gordon lifted the baby and laid it in April's waiting arms, the stained towel still tightly wrapped around it.

April gently opened the towel and looked down and then into Gordon's smiling face.

"Oh, Gordon, we have a son. We have a beautiful son," she whispered.

Gordon had perched on the bed next to April and their new son and he had never felt so relieved in his life. It was as if someone had removed great stones from his body that he had been forced to wear for the past eight months.

"How did this happen? How could we conceive a baby in Dreamville and bring him into the real world here at Burnock?" April asked.

Gordon shook his head and was about to say that he

had no idea when his cousin Sheila came running into the bedroom, followed by Mrs. MacCurdy.

"The ambulance is on the way . . ." Sheila had started to say when she saw the new family sitting on the bed, smiling and completely unaware that they were covered in blood.

Mrs. MacCurdy rushed from the room and returned with clean bedding to place under them where they sat as well as a soft cotton coverlet to wrap the baby in.

"Lady Stewart, I canna believe that the baby came so quickly. We barely had time to call the ambulance. Mr. Gordon has skills we dinna know of," she said.

Sheila held her arms out for the baby, which April reluctantly relinquished and watched as Gordon's cousin cleaned the baby, diapered him, and wrapped him in the clean swaddling cloth Mrs. MacCurdy had brought.

Mrs. MacCurdy had gone into the bathroom and returned with her arms full of soiled linens.

"I'll be taking these to the laundry while we wait for those louts driving the ambulance to take their own sweet taime," she said and left.

Sheila held the baby and smiled down at his sweet face. The baby suddenly reached his arms up toward

Sheila's face and she laughed in surprise before returning the child to his mother.

"I've never seen a newborn so alert. And he has not cried, has he? We thought you were still in labor because we had heard no crying baby yet."

Gordon shook his head again for what seemed like the hundredth time in the last few hours.

"Not a sound except for a few gurgles. I thought all new babies were supposed to cry," he said.

Sheila sat down on the opposite side of the bed next to April and could not help but touch the soft skin of her cousin's son's arm. They all heard the distant sounds of the ambulance making its way down the winding road to Burnock.

"Gordon, do I have to go to the hospital? I'm afraid to leave here, especially after . . ." she paused and looked at Sheila.

"Did something happen with Dreamville?" Sheila asked.

Both April and Gordon stared at Sheila.

"Well, yes. We've spent the last eight months there in the past, apart. We were at the hospital in New York when we found ourselves here."

Now it was Sheila's turn to shake her head.

"There's no way you could be there and here. You never went back to America. When April discovered she was pregnant, you stayed here. I only came up a few days ago to spend the last month of her pregnancy with you when the baby decided to come early."

"Wait, are you saying we never left Burnock?" Gordon asked.

The color had drained from both their faces and Sheila did not know what to say except what she knew to be true.

"Gordon, you two have never left. If you were here and in Dreamville, you . . . well, it makes no sense. April found out she was pregnant about a month after Alex died and the two of you married in the chapel with Samuel, Tamara, Sean, Andrew and myself as witnesses. There's no way you could have been in New York."

Mrs. MacCurdy's words to April echoed in Gordon's mind as Sheila described the events at Burnock during the last eight months.

He stared at April and saw the fear sweep across her face. Mrs. MacCurdy had called her Lady Stewart. She was now Pamela April Norris Stewart. Just as the stone in the family plot had been engraved in Dreamville.

Chapter Eleven

The drive to the small local hospital from Burnock had not been as fraught with pain and fear as the New York trip had been and once April and the baby were declared safe to travel, they and Gordon were airlifted to Edinburgh. Gordon wasn't entirely happy about the flight. He didn't think it necessary to transfer them to Edinburgh. They both seemed fine. And, he had to admit that a small part of him feared that April had been right in her desire not to leave Burnock.

Both she and the baby were declared healthy and strong, with the baby thriving with the love of his parents and the strong mother's milk that April's breasts seemed to produce in copious amounts. They spent only three days in Edinburgh before their return to Burnock. It was enough time for April to meet Sheila's girls and for Gordon's Edinburgh family to visit them, staring at the future Stewart laird through the window of the hospital's nursery.

Both sets of their parents called often and Gordon's father continued to ask medical questions and to tell Gordon what he should ask the doctors there to do. It was obvious to both new parents that the new grandparents would be visiting Scotland within the month. Gordon took many photos with his iPhone and messaged them to both their parents which only made their desire to see their young grandson even stronger.

They debated on names, but finally settled on naming him Ian Stewart, after the child's great-grandfather. They both agreed that it seemed only appropriate that, as Mrs. MacCurdy pronounced, the 'wee laird' be named after his forebears.

By the time they had returned to Burnock, over a week had passed and neither of them tried to think of the dire prediction that Dreamville had given Gordon so many months ago. Although almost a year had passed, the remembrance of the stone and the cairn next to it still haunted Gordon's every waking thought. April, too, thought of it, but managed to distract herself with the needs of their new son.

Mrs. MacCurdy and the new maid both tried to assist her, but she politely declined their offers and spent as much time with her son as possible. In the back of her mind, she subconsciously thought that she would not miss one second with him if something were to happen on January 8th.

On January 7th, Gordon became frantic with worry. He became surly and snapped at everyone. He was constantly alert for changes that only Dreamville could bring down upon them. He was terribly afraid that Will or Charlotte would show up and wreak havoc on their lives or that Dreamville would take them from him. He loved April so much that he could not imagine his life without her or his son.

At midnight on January 8th, he placed the baby between them in his larger bed and laid down next to them, placing his arm across them both, afraid of what might happen if he let go. By dawn, April had managed to calm him and get him to at least allow them some space on the bed.

"Are we to spend the entire day in your bed?" she

laughed.

"As long as we three are together, I can take it. What I cannot take is leaving the two of you and finding myself alone, not knowing where you are."

"Well, we can certainly spend the day in bed, but your son will need to nurse and have his diaper changed. And of course you and I will have to eat and make use of the bathroom at times," she replied.

Gordon rolled onto his back and looked at the ceiling when he remembered staring at the ceiling in the future Dreamville had shown him.

And that was when Will appeared at the foot of the bed, still dressed in his American prep clothes.

"I hope you've enjoyed your month with them, but I'm here to take Pamela back to where she belongs," he said and sneered at Gordon.

The baby suddenly screamed for the first time since he had been born and April held him close in fear of what Will had just said.

"What a noisy, bothersome brat. You can't take him, of course, Pamela. If that bastard hadn't taken you, you wouldn't have to worry about it anyway. This would have been over months ago," he said and pointed at Gordon.

"What do you mean 'taken me'?" April said.

"He took you away. I thought you were dead. Imagine my surprise when I found that he had pulled you into this 'world'. You were young then and I had to wait, but I did have so much fun tormenting that bastard as he grew up."

"No!" April screamed. "This is my world. I don't know who or what you are, but I am not your 'Pamela' and I'm not leaving. Ever!"

Will walked toward her and Gordon jumped across the bed to stop him, but the touch of Will's hand on Gordon's chest felt as if someone were crushing his heart and the light touch of Will's hand threw Gordon across the room.

"Put the child down or he'll end up worse than his father," Will said quietly. "As bothersome as he is, I am not completely without feeling. He can still live, unless you choose not do as I say."

Gordon was wheezing on the floor, trying to tell April to run, but she moved across the bed with her child and placed him in his father's arms.

"Take care of him for me, Gordon. I will always love you both and I will be back, but I can't let him hurt either of you and I think he can."

Gordon held his child as he watched his wife walk towards Will.

"April, please, no."

She looked back at them one more time and then simply faded with Will from the bedroom.

Chapter Twelve

Gordon regained his breath just as his wife vanished and he screamed her name so loudly that the entire household staff ran to his bedroom.

"He took her. He took her," was all he could get out as his infant son wailed.

"Someone took Lady Stewart?" Mrs. MacCurdy asked.

Gordon nodded as Ferguson helped him get to his feet while Gordon balanced his child against his chest.

"Oh my heavens, I'll call the police. Everyone go through the house. Maybe he hasn't gotten too far with Lady Stewart. Maybe they're still here in the house or on the estate grounds."

She barked the orders at the others who all rushed

from the room and were not really sure where to look or for whom they should look.

Gordon moved to the armchair next to the fireplace and rocked back and forth trying to comfort his son, but his son knew, just as he knew, that April would not be found anywhere on the grounds of Burnock.

Sean arrived about 30 minutes later with men from the village to search the grounds and the local roads for any sign of a strange man or Lady Stewart.

"Gordon, who is this man? I know you. You would never have let someone take her while you were in the room. You have to tell me everything," Sean said.

Gordon described most of the event, but out of necessity left out the parts which Sean would never understand and might even make Sean think that Gordon had done something to April or worse yet was insane as Alexander had called him.

"I just don't get how this American could overpower you and I seriously can't see April allowing anyone to take her away from your baby."

Gordon had earlier placed the crying baby in his crib as the child seemed inconsolable. The baby had continued to cry until Mrs. MacCurdy had come watch over him and had comforted him while Gordon tried to talk with Sean.

"Sean, damn it, the man attacked me first, then threatened to kill me and the baby unless April went with him. I tried to stop him!"

At this point, Gordon ripped his shirt so hard that the buttons went flying through the air like errant missiles. Beneath the shirt and over his heart was a dark black bruise in the shape of a large hand.

"Look! This is what he did to me. I thought he would kill me, but still I fought him. I tried. Do you think I would have ever let anyone hurt April?"

Gordon sat down and covered his face as if shamed by his actions. Sean walked over and put his hand on Gordon's shoulder. He honestly felt pain for his life long friend. He knew that this was killing Gordon.

"I'm sorry, Gordon. I had to ask. You know. I believe you, but I still had to ask. Do you want me to call anyone in your family?"

Gordon thought of Sheila and their respective families, but decided that needed to be done by him and no one else. He shook his head and clasped his hands in front of his face, his elbows propped upon his knees.

"Nae, I'll make the calls. Just please find her. Please."

"We're working, Gordon, but I need you to give your statement to one of the officers and have someone photograph that bruise. We also need to inspect your room. I'm sorry."

Sean left the room to speak with two officers he was stationing at Burnock while everyone else combed the estate grounds and the lands around Burnock and to have the officers do the forensic examinations.

After the policeman was finished with him, Gordon called Sheila first and she said she would be there as soon as possible. He telephoned her from the study to prevent being overheard as he told her everything that happened, including Will's cryptic comments.

"Oh, Gordon, I'm so sorry. No, no, it canna be," she stopped and took a deep breath to try and not fall apart at what Gordon had just told her. She felt as if her entire world were being turned upside down. She finally caught her breath and began to speak again.

"Gordon, he was pure evil. I knew that the first time he appeared. I had hoped he was gone forever. I just don't understand how he could "take" her. Where? It makes no sense. People don't just vanish like that?"

"Yes, Sheila. They do or they did, at least in what April

called Dreamville. One minute they were there and the next gone."

"I'll call Andrew and leave as soon as possible. At least I can tell him the truth, though he won't be happy. What I mean to say is that he will worry about protecting me, especially if you couldn't save April, I mean, oh bloody hell, I'm making no sense whatsoever. Don't give up, Gordon. We'll find them. We'll find out where he took her."

He thanked her, hung up the phone and then picked up the phone again, this time to call his parents and then April's family. He had no doubt that they would all be on planes bound for Scotland as soon as possible.

Their reactions to the news was exactly as he had thought it would be – confusion, fear, devastation, and feeling completely helpless – all things he was experiencing himself.

He saw that the sun was high in the sky and realized that the baby would be getting hungry. He leapt from his seat and bounded up the stairs to find his son. Mrs. MacCurdy had already gotten a bottle of April's milk for the baby and was preparing to feed him when Gordon entered the yellow bedroom.

He smiled at his son, took him from Mrs. MacCurdy

and cradled him in his arms. The child clasped at the bottle, but moved one hand to cover his father's long fingers.

"We'll find her," Gordon whispered to his son. "I swear to you I'll bring her home to you."

The baby pinched his father's fingers and looked up at him.

Mrs. MacCurdy left them there in the sunny yellow room, wondering just how Lady Stewart disappeared with a stranger. It wasn't that she didn't believe Gordon's narration of events. She just felt that something about it was not right.

Gordon spent the rest of the afternoon sitting in a rocking chair next to the crib, holding his son and missing his wife. The baby gurgled and grabbed his finger, refusing to let go. His son fell asleep holding onto Gordon, who felt as if the two of them were robbed, abandoned, and left desolate by April's disappearance. He thought of the baby's screams when Will had appeared. The baby rarely cried, but when Will appeared it was as if he knew Will was evil. It was strange and he wished he knew what his child was thinking.

The sun was beginning to set when Sheila arrived and entered the bedroom where Gordon still sat with his son.

She paused for a moment before making her presence known. She had never seen a moment in time so beautiful and so sad in her life – the baby's sleeping head against Gordon's white shirted shoulder and Gordon forlornly staring out the window. The entire room glowed yellow from the setting sun and the color of the wallpaper. If not for the agony that her cousin was suffering, it would be a timeless painting of father and child.

"Gordon, let me take the baby. He needs changed and fed. And you need to eat as well. No matter what happens you have to live for your son."

Gordon handed the baby over to Sheila and stood and looked out the window at the crowd of people from town who had spent the day looking for April and Will. But they won't find her, he thought. He knew she wasn't in this world. She was wherever Dreamville had allowed Will to take her.

"How could she do it? How could she leave us?" he said angrily.

"Oh Gordon, did she have a choice? If everything you told me happened, he left her no choice. If I had to choose between the lives of Andrew and my girls and going with a madman, I would have done the same."

"She didn't leave you. He took her. We just need to find out where," she continued as she finished changing the baby's diaper.

Gordon walked away from the window and went to the door to go down to see if Sean had any news, though he knew Sean would not.

"But how do we find her? How do we find a place that exists outside of our world?" he stopped and said before leaving the room.

Sheila shook her head as he left and put the baby down in the crib while she waited for Mrs. MacCurdy to bring a bottle of April's milk for the baby. She thought of April's milk and wondered how much April had put in reserve for the baby. If the baby no longer had April's milk, he would have to make the transition to formula.

Sheila watched the people outside and wiped a tear from her cheek. It didn't seem fair, but she understood April's choice. Any mother would have made the same choice, she thought.

Outside, Gordon walked over to where Sean was talking with the people who had spent the day looking for April and her abductor. When Sean saw Gordon, the look on his face told Gordon everything – no luck, no tracks, no trace.

"Gordon, we'll start looking again in the morning, but we've had no luck today. I've contacted other police departments and there's now a nationwide notice of April's abduction. Surely, someone will have seen her or the American."

Gordon smiled weakly and nodded his head.

"I'd like to thank everyone who has helped. I should have tried harder to resist him. I should have fought harder . . ."

"He almost killed you and you had the baby in your arms. Don't blame yourself. We'll find her," Sean said. What he did not tell Gordon was that he was afraid that the American had done something to April and that she might never be found. But he had to give his friend hope right now. Later, Gordon could come to terms with the truth of his loss.

Chapter Thirteen

April found herself walking into a house in New Haven and was surprised that Will would take her back to America where her family was, where Gordon's family was.

She stared at the house, finding that it was the home of a rich man, a house modeled on an English Tudor, with large rooms, luxurious furnishings and fixtures. Was Will, or Jon Williams, or whoever he was, that rich? And how did he come to know her? How did she fit into this?

She stopped and stood still in the large foyer and refused to move any further, waiting for him to turn to her and give her some reason why she had been ripped from the arms of the people she loved.

Will turned and saw her stubborn attempt to assert herself.

"Pamela that will do no good. You are here. You are never going back. Only I found the way the transitions work and I can stop them from happening again. Now be the good wife you were and obey me."

April looked puzzled and confused. Obey him? Be his good wife?

Will sighed and remembered that she could not know how things were with his Pamela. He had waited ten years for this and he was determined to have his wife back, even if she was from another place or time or was someone else.

"You do not understand how things are between us, but you will. We were, we are husband and wife, long before you met that Stewart brat in your version of life. But here in my world, you belong to me."

"I will explain more of it, but not yet. You're not ready. Now, you must understand one thing. I can destroy your other world completely. I'm sure you do not want me to travel to Burnock and hurt someone important to you."

"You bastard. You wouldn't. If you even think of doing something so cruel, I'll end this before it starts. I'd sooner take my own life than live on your terms."

Will was shocked by the vehemence in her voice. His Pamela had never spoken to him in such a manner.

"Do not use that tone with me or threaten me. My wife does not do such things. I will not be embarrassed by your behavior."

"I don't know what kind of woman your 'Pamela' was, but I am not her. I only came because I thought you were going to hurt my family. But take my word, if you even think of using that to control me, it won't work. Do you understand? I'd sooner die than allow you to hold something like that over my head!"

"Pamela, you must . . ."

April picked up a vase from a side table and threw it in the floor between them, shattering it.

"I am not Pamela. I am April. I am here because you used fear to get me here, but even if I can't find a way back, I'd sooner be homeless than 'obey' you," she spat out.

He rushed across the foyer, the glass from the vase crunching under his leather shoes. He had his hand around her throat, just under her jaw and squeezed.

"You, my dear, will obey me. If you want that brat of yours to live. You will live with me as my wife and do everything I say. You will do no harm to yourself nor to me. You see, if you do, I have a back up plan to destroy your little family," he said as he squeezed her throat harder.

"Charlotte, you can come out now," he called out. He was holding April's neck so tightly that she could barely keep her feet on the ground.

The white enamel doors on the right side of the foyer slid apart and April saw to her horror that Charlotte had been there the entire time, waiting for Will to signal her entrance.

She looked at the fear in April's face and began to laugh.

"Will, darling, I'll never understand your fascination with this creature. She's nothing like Pamela other than her looks."

"Shut up, Charlotte. She is the same Pamela, just from a different world."

He turned back to April.

"What do you call it? Dreamville?"

April was unable to reply and her face was turning blue from his hand about her throat. He immediately released her and she fell to the floor in a heap, struggling to avoid the shards of the Chinese vase and trying to regain her breath.

Charlotte walked over to Will and put her arm around his waist and smiled.

"Whatever you say, darling, as long as she doesn't interfere with our fun or plans."

Will removed Charlotte's hand from his waist and let it drop as if it were diseased.

"Not now, Charlotte. Take her to the bedroom and lock the door. I have some things to take care of here before we begin."

Charlotte grabbed April's elbow and shoved her up the staircase and April could not help but be reminded of the awful events of the version of Dreamville where her family and she had been murdered. She felt a chill run through her body and Charlotte almost had to drag her up the staircase.

Charlotte pushed her into a bedroom furnished with fine New England antiques. She pointed to a machine on the dresser that April recognized and almost cried in despair.

"Use the breast pump to rid your tits of the milk building up in them. You no longer have any use for it and it only disgusts Will. Pour the milk in the sink, rinse the sink and the pump and clean yourself. You do not want him to smell it on you."

April sat down upon the side of the bed and looked

around for any hope she might have of escaping from this nightmare into which she had been thrust.

"Another bit of advice, dearie. Do as he says. Obey him and do not fight him. He will make you regret it," Charlotte added as she left the room.

April could hear the key locking the door and she stood and began to search for a way to escape. Will had said that he knew the secret to the 'transitions' between worlds. She believed that if he could figure them out then she could as well. She decided her priority was to discover how to return home, to her reality, her place and time.

Unfortunately, she realized that that meant playing his game, pretending to do what he asked, and god help her, do worse if necessary.

She could feel her breast beginning to fill with milk and she used the pump to remove and dispose of her baby's food. She cried as she the milk swirled round in circles in the basin and down the sink trap. She thought of the waste of the nourishment her child needed and wailed as her son had when she followed Will. She dropped to her knees on the oiled hard wood maple floor, one pale hand draped over the white porcelain basin. She wept until her eyes could produce no more tears than her breasts could produce milk for her son so far away.

Finally, after she had calmed herself, after she completed the ritual by cleaning the electric pump and putting it back on the lowboy, she went back to the bathroom and washed her face. She hoped that Will would not return for her and see that she had been crying. She wanted to give him no evidence of weakness.

Just as Sheila was taking care of her baby and helping Gordon, April sat on the bed and buried deep in her heart all the pain she felt as she waited for Will to reappear to torture her further. No matter what he did to her, she would always belong to Gordon and their son, she thought. She would never give up hope of returning to their loving arms.

Chapter Fourteen

It was not Will who unlocked and opened the door, but Charlotte.

"Come, bitch, time to dine. I assume you have removed that odious liquid and cleaned yourself of the smell of it. And remember – no misbehavior. Trust me. I know what he can do to you and those you love."

April stood still and stared at Charlotte.

"What do you mean? Did he do something to you? Did he hurt you?"

Charlotte laughed and grabbed April, pushing her from the room.

"Of course, he took me from Gordon and brought you into all of our lives. You have no idea how you ruined my life."

"But Charlotte, I didn't know you. I didn't know how Gordon felt. I knew none of it. Why allow Will to punish both of us for something we've never done."

"Oh you bloody fool. He interfered in my relationship with Gordon and pushed Gordon back into your arms. Gordon would never take me back now, especially not with the little bastard you presented him."

"Enough," Charlotte said. "Get downstairs. Will is waiting in the dining room for both us. Oh, and don't try to get the servants to help. They'll just think you're crazy. At least they think that's where you've been the last years, in a sanitarium. Don't mention anything about your other life around them or he'll make you regret it."

Before Charlotte moved toward the staircase she stopped and almost spat at April.

"If I can't have Gordon, you bloody well can't either. I hate Will as much as you do, but I hate you more. You tore the only love I had from my arms," she finished and pushed April through the hall.

April stumbled down the steps and found Charlotte directing her into the room across from where Charlotte had emerged earlier.

The dining room was styled in American Federal

replete with late 18th century furnishings and accoutrements. Will was sitting at the head of the table, casually dressed for a table so formally laid out. He gestured for April to sit at the opposite end of the table and Charlotte pushed April into the seat before moving to her own seat in the center of the table.

Without a word an older woman entered and began to serve the meal, placing filled plates before each of them onto chargers. Behind her another woman followed and decanted wine into their goblets and just as quickly as they had entered, they were gone through a swinging door painted Federal Blue to match the painted wood trim in the room.

April sat and stared at the food as if at any moment it would dissolve into the ethereal realm of Dreamville and she would be back once more with Gordon and their son. She began to tear up and fought the emotions that threatened to overwhelm her. How can I eat, she thought. Somewhere her family was waiting, looking for her.

Will noticed her lack of movement and directed her to begin her meal.

"Not eating will not return you to that place. This is your home as it has been for the entirety of our marriage.

Your behavior is becoming very tiresome. Do not force me to punish you."

April looked to Charlotte, who was eating quite heartily and seeming to enjoy April's discomfiture. April realized that she was wearing the red dress that Gordon and Sheila had described from their sighting of her at both Burnock and New York.

April became furious that Charlotte seemed to enjoy her misery and she was tired of Will's threats. Nothing could be as miserable as being forced to be his 'wife'.

"You will do nothing of the sort. In fact, you are not my husband and you cannot control me," she said tersely and stood and left the room, heading to the front door. She was in New Haven and she was only a town or two away from her parents. They, at least, would save her from having to remain in this monster's house.

Before she could open the front door, Will had moved quickly around her and blocked her exit from his home. He took her right upper arm and squeezed it tightly enough to bruise it. She noticed that here he could not move as quickly as he had in her real world. For the first time she had hope. He might not be invincible here. She might be able to actually escape him.

"I said you would do as I say, Pamela, or you will be punished. I see that your recalcitrance is much worse than it was when we first married. Well, I cured you of it then and I shall again. Now, upstairs," he said and shoved her towards the winding staircase.

She tried to fight back, but his hold on her arm was too strong. She tried to kick at him, but he dodged every movement as if he knew exactly what she was about to do before she did it. He began to ascend the stairs, half dragging her behind him. She began to be afraid of what his intentions were once they reached the second floor and she began to pull away from him frantically, even falling to her knees and almost losing her balance on the steps.

None of it helped. By the time they reached the room she had been locked into earlier, he threw her into the room and she landed hard on the floor, the Aubusson carpet barely softening her fall. He leaned over her and began to slap her face as she crawled backwards trying to escape his blows.

But just as quickly as he began to strike her, he stopped.

"You'll remain here until you can behave properly. For every meal you miss, you will be beaten. I will not allow this to continue. You will obey me."

He moved closer to her, his face only inches away from her face. She could smell the strong odor of wine on his breath.

"You must understand. You have nowhere to go. Your family does not exist here. That man is not here to rescue you and if you managed to find him, he would not know you. He has never known you. As April you might one day have found him, but you are Pamela here, my wife and mentally unstable after the murders of your family."

April gasped. The Dreamville deaths of her family flashed through her mind.

"Yes, they're all gone. You were the only survivor, though we thought you dead at first. Luckily I discovered you in the other place and told everyone here that you were in a sanitarium. I had to wait for the right time to bring you back home and that time has finally arrived."

He stood over her and straightened his clothing and ran his hand through his blond hair, smoothing it down.

"I told you once that only I knew how to move between the places and you will never know. Forget about everything you thought you knew. This is your life now. This is your only world. 'Dreamville' is everything you thought you knew."

He walked out the door, closed and locked it, leaving her lying on the rug in the light entering the darkened room from the streetlamp outside. She struggled to her knees and remembered the incident in the bedroom at Burnock where Will had appeared in a dark bedroom lit only by a street light. That was the instance where Sheila had found her, and then Gordon and Andrew.

"Oh, Gordon, where are you?" she cried out.

She could not live like this. She would rather die than live in Will's world. If this was where Dreamville had deposited her, it would be the last.

She stood and looked out the window at the street below. It was damp and dark and empty as it had been the night of Alex's funeral. She leaned her forehead against the glass and felt almost an electric shock. She stood back from it and stared at the pane and almost miraculously she saw Gordon sitting in the moonlight cradling their son. She touched the window again and felt the electric quiver of the glass as if it were a semi-liquid barrier between this world and her world.

At first she thought of throwing herself through the window and then she paused and thought of Will and

Charlotte downstairs. If this were truly their world, then they might be able to be stopped here if nowhere else. If she somehow managed to return to Gordon, she could not take the chance that Will and Charlotte would come for her or her family. She had to come up with a solid plan before attempting to leap through that glass.

And then there was the other problem – leaping through the glass could be a mirage of her tortured mind and it could kill her. But it could also take her somewhere else, including her home at Burdock. Anywhere but here.

So she stepped back from the window and looked at the locked door. She would end this forever even if meant murdering the two people who kept her captive, even if meant that running through that window might end her own life. Either way, she didn't care. She may have found Will's secret of moving between the dimensions of the different paths life took each of them. Her task was to accommodate only his modest needs, giving her the chance to stop him. She would be strong. Although the image of Gordon and her son was fading from the window pane, she felt hope for the first time in years. She might actually be able to rid them of Dreamville by destroying the person who had begun it all ten years ago. She closed her eyes and smiled, knowing that no matter what happened when she finally flew through that window and landed, Gordon and her baby would be safe from Will and Charlotte forever.

Chapter Fifteen

"Sean, it's been almost a week and you've found nothing?" Sheila asked as they drank tea in the parlor at Burnock. She glanced around the room and realized that it was only a year ago she had sat here mourning the loss of Alex. Damn the bastard who had taken him from them, she thought.

Sean shook his head before taking a sip of the hot tea. His hands were almost clumsy with the delicate tea cup and she wished she had just made the tea herself rather than have Mrs. MacCurdy serve them tea.

"It makes no sense. Two Americans in the Highlands would be noticed, especially someone such as Lady Stewart, whose face has been in the tabloids. Actually April's face is so well known in both Scotland and Britain that someone should have seen her. Even if he had help smuggling her out of Scotland, someone should have noticed something."

He sighed before he continued. He had to tell someone in the family the truth, no matter how difficult. Sheila seemed to be the strongest of all of them. Samuel was preoccupied with having left Tamara alone in Edinburgh and Alexander's mother hadn't even bothered to make an appearance, but Sean wasn't surprised by her actions. She had made it quite clear that she despised April. Sean was sure that she was the source of all the tabloid articles that had swirled around them when Alex had shot himself.

He also knew that Gordon's and April's families would be arriving in the morning and someone had to talk to Gordon before they came to Burnock. Gordon had to be prepared for the worst so that he could prepare their families.

"The other answer is that he took her into the mountains and . . . and harmed her," he said to Sheila.

"Oh Sean, no. We can't think that, much less utter it. I don't think Gordon could survive that. He's barely able to hold himself together as it is."

"Sheila, we've all tried to help. The village, the local families, everyone has spent the last week searching for her, not just here but in the rest of the island to no avail. We've found not a trace. I wish I had better news. I just wanted to stop by and see how he was faring and ask you to help me prepare him for the worst."

He sighed and rubbed his temples.

"I still canna believe this has happened."

He finished the tea and stood to leave.

"Please let him know that I called and that we've not given up the search. But, you will have to eventually mention the Highland search for a body. I don't want to distress him with that, but he has to be ready."

Sheila smiled sadly and thanked Sean for his help. She watched his retreating back as he left Burnock and poured another cup of tea for herself. She wished she could tell Sean about Dreamville, about the Will creature, but she knew he would think her mad. Both Gordon and Andrew had warned her not to discuss it. But she wondered if telling him might help.

No, she thought, Gordon and Andrew were right. This talk of other dimensions, other worlds, of someplace called Dreamville could not help return April to her home and possibly could make things much worse for Gordon.

There was also the puzzling question of the overlapping year in which young Ian had been conceived with his parents separated in one time and yet together here at Burnock. Could these dimensions that Gordon had mentioned last year have overlapped enough that variations of Gordon and April had lived in both places simultaneously?

She shook her head, confused by the idea of such a thing, gathered the tea cups onto the tray and carried it back into the kitchen where Mrs. MacCurdy had been sitting waiting for Sheila to signal for her.

"Oh Miss Sheila, you should not be doing my work. Mr. Gordon needs your assistance much more than I do," and she took the tray from Sheila and began to remove the contents of the tray.

Sheila smiled at her and felt her smile slip away as she went back through the quiet house that tomorrow would be filled with worried, weeping and tormented family members. God help us all, she thought. Please let April be safe and come home soon.

Chapter Sixteen

Gordon moved from his bedroom into the yellow bedroom where his son slept. He, too, slept there in the bed he had shared with his love. Sometimes at night he talked aloud to April, hoping that wherever the Will creature had taken her that she might hear him, even if only in her sleep where she might be allowed to dream of being with Gordon and her son.

Sometimes, when the moon hung low above the craggy highlands and shone into the yellow bedroom, before he opened his eyes and knew the truth, he could almost feel the heat of her body in the sheets next to him, feel her body moving beneath the sheets and smell the strong scent of her. He would whisper her name and hear her soft breathing.

He would struggle in his sleep to find her on those nights, knowing that she was there and then waking in the moonlight to find her side of the bed empty and cold. Raising himself upon his elbows, his mouth would be dry and he would fight to breathe when he realized that it was untrue, that he had been merely dreaming.

Outside, the moon cast comforting and familiar shadows over the grounds of Burnock and he would go to the window and touch the cool window pane with his fingers, somehow feeling that the sheet of glass was the only thing separating him from April. On those nights, he would turn and look around the room and remember the quilt that April had made of the room in their last version of Dreamville. The yellow flocked wallpaper almost glittered in the moonlight the way the citrines had glowed on the quilt. He would remember the two of them dancing in the pale light from the window on one of her last nights with them there, their small son cradled between them, their hearts as full of love as any two people could be.

Of course, after a few minutes reality would tear those ghosts of the pasts from his sleep deprived mind and he would see the room as the cold and empty place it really was, with just him and his small son who silently watched his father from the crib that stood next to the window.

The child never cried, had never cried or even cooed any sounds other than the tortured cries he had emitted when his mother was pulled away from him that horrible night. Now the infant and his father silently waited and watched, hoping that April was not really a ghost, but the one love they shared who had just gone away for a short time.

Some nights Mrs. MacCurdy would find him sleep walking through the house, examining each window, surprised to find that he held a small dagger in his hand as he searched the house for April. When she told Sheila the first time she had found him in the front parlor, stripped bare to the waist and his body tensed as if ready to confront whatever demons his dreams brought him, she was surprised that Sheila was not shocked.

"He's looking for her. He looks everywhere. In his sleep, in his walks about the grounds and the churchyard. No, I'm not surprised that he would look for her in his sleep. He has lost everything he held dear except his son."

Sheila and Mrs. MacCurdy had become close over the past few months since she had first come to help with the birth and had returned to help care for Gordon and his son after April's disappearance. After a short time they dropped the formalities of the servant and guest and had joined one another as friends whose only care was that Gordon survive to see April again.

Of course, Sheila never told Mrs. MacCurdy of Dreamville. She knew no way to explain it to the woman who was unknowingly succumbing to the stress of the situation by aging a decade in months. Where before Mrs. MacCurdy's hair had been a mixture of salt and pepper, it was now almost snow white. Sheila feared for the woman's health, but she never mentioned it as she sometimes believed that the woman's need to help was one of the few things that kept her and the cook strong.

Ferguson, who had served the family for decades as their driver, could finally no longer take the heartbreak that pervaded the house. He was a pragmatist first and foremost. He believed that Lady Stewart had been taken into the Highlands surrounding Burnock and most likely murdered. He could not bear to see the hope that each day faded from the faces of the family in the house. After several weeks, he gave his notice and went to his son's home in Aberdeen where he had decided to live out his days and not think of whatever fate had overtaken the young Laird's wife.

Gordon was not surprised when the new maid had brought her young man from the village to apply for Ferguson's position. That he was called Craig by Gordon before the young maid had introduced him by his Christian name surprised the young couple, but they said nothing. They were simply grateful to have found positions in the same household that allowed them the chance to marry and one day possibly have their own family.

To Gordon, everything was occurring as it had in his horrible visit to Burnock in the future. The only difference was that he had not been aware that he and April had had a child. Fate or Dreamville or whatever dimensional theory of time and worlds he could think of had only given some certain glimpses of only one of many futures and he feared the day he remembered from his prior trip when he was older and he had discovered that April's remains had been found neath the trestle bridge near the depot at Edinburgh.

He also struggled with whether or not to tell Sheila what he little he knew of Andrew's fate. His cousin Sheila, the staff who were as much family and friends as anyone, were the only people he felt he could trust once his own parents and April's family had returned to America. Even they had given up hope that she would be found alive. It was Sheila who broached the subject first with him at Sean's urging and he finally had to admit to their extended family that April might be lost to them forever.

Chapter Seventeen

Gordon chose not to tell Sheila of Andrew's premature death. If anyone could be happy, let it be she and Andrew. The knowledge of Andrew's death could do nothing but harm to his beloved cousin and her children.

Sheila would take a few days here and there to return to Edinburgh to see to her own household duties and her own family and had not Andrew needed to remain at his job there, she would have brought her daughters Emily and Cameron and her husband back to Burnock to stay there with her. She missed them horribly, but she and Andrew had discussed it repeatedly. He believed that April would return very soon and so he would bring their daughters to Burnock almost every weekend to see their mother and stay till Sunday evening when he would take them back to the city and their school and friends.

When Sheila and Mrs. MacCurdy had sat in the kitchen at the long trestle table drinking tea and talking of Gordon's dilemma, she had no idea that she was echoing another of April's quilts from Manhattan. But Gordon began to see the patterns from the quilts in their everyday life at Burnock and it concerned him that April might have been unknowingly trying to warn him of what Burnock could become.

Sheila would think of her own family and ache for them. She would then think of Gordon's loss, his not knowing, his waiting alone with his son, both waiting for a wife and mother who might never return and Sheila would almost weep in despair. At least she knew her family was safe in Edinburgh and that she would see them on weekends. Gordon did not even have that.

The girls, on the other hand, loved the trips to Burnock and were waiting by the door at their house in Edinburgh for their father's return from work, luggage packed and ready to leave the minute he arrived. He laughed at their eager anticipation of seeing their mother and how they enjoyed riding the grounds of Burnock or the trips into the village where the residents had adopted them as their own.

He only feared that what he had seen the one time at Burnock might befall them as well, but he never mentioned it to Sheila and especially not to Gordon. Gordon's pain was so evident, so tangible, that he could never begrudge Gordon what family he had left.

As the year progressed and the cold Highland spring turned into summer, Andrew and Gordon would sit in the garden watching the girls and their mother riding in the distance. The baby was growing quickly and by summer's end was beginning to try to walk. Gordon would place his large hand at the small of his son's back and carefully helping him to step around the garden bench.

"He's growing fast, Gordon," Andrew remarked one afternoon as they watched from the garden Sheila and the girls riding in the distance near the burn.

Gordon thought again of one of April's quilts – The Burn and he wondered if this view had anything to do with bringing her back to him and Ian. He smiled at his son and waved at the girls in the distance.

"Aye, as are your girls. Thank you for allowing Sheila to stay here. I only hope you feel as welcome here as she and your daughters do."

Andrew smiled wryly, thinking of the wasted anger that had passed between them last year. Sheila and the girls loved Burnock more than he would have ever thought and it comforted him that he knew they would always have a home there if they needed it.

Andrew had not told his family or Gordon that he had developed a heart problem and that he feared he would not live to see his own children grow up. While it would be several years before Andrew died at his desk at work one midday, Gordon always blamed himself afterwards for not having told Andrew what Dreamville had revealed to him. He would later wonder if Andrew would have survived if he had known or received better care.

Gordon looked down at Ian and watched as his son let go of the bench and take steps away from it and slowly toddle toward the arched garden entrance when the garnet colored roses bloomed. Ian had just taken his first steps alone and April, wherever she was, had been robbed of one the most important rites of motherhood.

Chapter Eighteen

While April's young son was growing quickly and searching for her in his own strange and eerie way that only a toddler could, April's time in Will and Charlotte's world was passing unbearably slowly. It was as if time had come to a crawl since she had discovered the window pane and seen her husband and small Ian sitting in the rocker in the yellow bedroom, looking into the distant mountains.

She had not approached the window again since that night as she both was afraid that it had simply been a hope created by her deluded and lonely heart or a dangerous door into a world that might not even lead back to her family.

Each day was repeated in monotonous detail. She would wake, remove her child's nourishment from her body, bathe to remove the smell of him from her body and be led to the dining room for a breakfast that was silent on her part and yet lively and talkative on the part of her captors.

She would eat, answer Will's questions, and submerge the anger and hatred that almost choked her and kept her from responding to him. After a few weeks, she had become quite an actress and thought that maybe Will was starting to believe that she had come to accept her fate there. She dreaded more than anything that he might find her act so believable that he would try to rejoin what had once been a marriage bed with the woman called Pamela, the woman she was not and had never been.

But she could tell by Charlotte's watchful eyes that Charlotte did not believe the act. Charlotte would push the buttons that caused April the most pain – how Gordon was living without her, how her family had dealt with her disappearance and possible death, and worst of all, how her son would grow up motherless and lonely. Charlotte just kept picking at her, never letting her forget everything April had given up by staying in Will's home, locked in a bedroom alone except for being allowed to come to the dining room for meals.

April sat in the dark bedroom each night watching the window pane and praying that she might just be given one small glimpse of her husband and son. Some nights the window glass seemed to waver, but then would just as quickly stop. Nothing seemed real to her anymore and she knew she had to escape before she did become irredeemably insane from sorrow and loss.

And just as she thought she could no longer bear the horror of her situation, Will finally allowed her to join him and Charlotte in the living room after supper one night. He was in a jolly mood and he put her next to him on the long green sofa embroidered with gold Napoleonic bees. He wrapped his arm behind her and although his touch made her nauseous, she smiled shyly and tried to be as good an actress as Meryl Streep.

Charlotte sat across from them sipping from a brandy snifter and frowning at what she saw happening. She knew April was pretending and she had told Will exactly that, but Will was so eager to have his Pamela back that he ignored her protests.

It was then that Charlotte did her utmost to separate April from Gordon and Ian. She convinced Will that 'Pamela' should take a pill that would dry up her breast milk and rid her of the last vestiges of her connection to that other world of which she would not let go. Will thought it was a brilliant idea. If Pamela were no longing producing milk for a child that did not exist in his world, he would be able to approach her as only a husband could – sexually.

When April found a blue pill next to her water glass the next morning at breakfast, she was puzzled and Charlotte gleefully explained what the pill was for. It took every ounce of her emotional strength to smile at both Will and Charlotte and swallow the pill. It had only been three weeks that she had been there and her breast milk was her last connection to Ian, but she knew that if she were to escape from this nightmare world, she had to convince both of them that she was ready to leave her true husband and son for this charade of a marriage Will believed to be real.

After Charlotte had returned her to her room and loudly locked the door, April almost threw up the contents of her stomach, but she knew the loss of the milk was a small price to pay so she continued to take the pills and after two more weeks, she no longer needed the breast pump and her breasts, returned to their normal shape, were no longer sore or full of the ache to feed her child.

Now if she could only avoid Will's stronger sexual desires and still gain his trust, she might actually be close enough to fight him, to fight Charlotte and return to her life.

It was the night that her milk had finally dissipated, that she sat next to Will on the green sofa and suddenly felt his hand moving through the long strands of her hair.

"This mess will have to be cut off, you know Pamela. You're not a teenager and short cropped hair always suited you better."

Charlotte smiled over her glass of scotch this time and waited for April's response. Charlotte was quite surprised to see April smile back at her.

April turned to Will and smiled at him as well.

"Of course, Will. You're absolutely right. But how can I get a decent cut without leaving the house? Do you trust me enough to let me out?"

He chuckled and pulled a pair of shears from his inside blazer pocket and handed them over to Charlotte.

"No need for that dear. Charlotte can do it quite well, though perhaps we should adjourn to the downstairs bath for your shearing. Wouldn't want to get hair all over the living room."

April took a deep breath and stood.

"Well then, let's get it done. I'll have to wash and dry my hair to get the loose hairs that stick to my skin off."

"Splendid!" Will said and joined her to lead her to the bathroom.

Charlotte was very skeptical of this. Gordon loved April's hair and she found it hard to believe that April would allow herself to be sheared like a sheep. She finished her drink in a quick gulp and followed Will and April where Will had already prepared a chair and apron for his 'Pamela'.

When the first long tress fell to the paper under the chair, April swallowed the nausea that filled her gut and smiled. If she could give up her son's milk, she could give up her hair. It could always grow back if she could make it back to her world.

It took almost 30 minutes for Charlotte to cut her hair without making her look as if she truly had been sheared like a whore with lice. Charlotte knew exactly the cut Will wanted. He had shown Charlotte a picture of his real Pamela and had told Charlotte to cut it precisely as it was in the photograph. The difference was that his Pamela had

had straight hair and April's hair, even after being cut, still retained its curl.

He became angry with Charlotte and grabbed the shears from her hand.

"Did you do that on purpose, to try to make her ugly and unattractive to me? It was a simple cut. You are absolutely useless!"

April began to tremble in the chair, afraid of what Will might do to her with the shears, but she saw the same fear in Charlotte's face.

"Will, darling, her hair is curly and your Pamela's hair was straight . . ."

He slapped Charlotte hard enough to knock her into the door frame. He walked around April and stood as close as possible to Charlotte as he could.

"This is my Pamela," he hissed.

"Of course, Will, I'm sorry. I'll do better next time," Charlotte whimpered in the face of his anger.

His body relaxed and he looked over his shoulder at April, his mouth forming a smile, but his eyes still filled with rage.

"Yes, dear Charlotte, but it won't be necessary."

He shoved the long shears into her belly and up into

her chest, the whole time looking at April. Charlotte slid down the doorframe silently, her death that quick and April remembered how the person who appeared to be Gordon had shot her in the same manner in the darkest corner of Dreamville.

She tried not to show any emotion on her face, but she could not help but feel sorry for Charlotte. For all of Charlotte's wickedness, she had not deserved to die because April had curly hair and Will's dead wife had had straight.

"Well, Pamela, you go ahead and go take your shower. I'll dispose of this mess. I can trust you not to try to leave, can't I?"

April nodded and slid next to the wall, stepping over the pool of blood that was forming on the floor where Charlotte's body lie. She saw that Charlotte was wearing that red dress she had worn the first night and she shivered. No matter what world or place or dimension she was in, Charlotte always died the same way. By the time she was in the hall, April ran up the staircase and had never been so happy to be in that accursed bedroom.

As she undressed in the dark bedroom, she noticed the pane of glass in the window wavering and for the first time in weeks she saw Gordon and Ian, this time in the garden at Burnock with Andrew. She watched as Ian took his first steps towards the arch and shoved her fist into her mouth to keep from crying in joy. Her most precious son had just taken his first steps and the window pane had given her the gift of seeing him. While she realized that time in her own world was passing faster, she knew now, somehow, someway, that in just a few short weeks, she could be home with her family.

Chapter Nineteen

April was awakened by Will shaking her shoulders. She was suddenly afraid that he had come to claim her as his wife when he started pulling at her rings on her hand. His skin was rough and felt crusted with dirt. Even in the dim light from the hall she could see they were stained dark, almost black.

"Give me your wedding rings and jewelry. By the time they find Charlotte's body in Scotland, nothing will be left but a few bones and your jewelry. Perfect way to make Gordon think you're dead. We'll kill two birds with one stone so to speak. She'll be there and everyone will think her bones are yours and you'll be here with me."

"Yes, perfection!" he exclaimed.

April soundlessly allowed him to take her jewelry. He

was so excited with his tasks that he paid her no heed, which was good because his taking some of the last items she had from her world with Gordon hurt more than anything had short of his taking her from Gordon and Ian. He was so involved in telling her his plans and removing her rings that he did not notice that this time she could not hide the devastating effect the removal of the ring had caused.

She realized just how insane he was as he talked on and on about tricking Gordon and having finally rid them both of Charlotte. That was when April knew that no matter what transpired or how she felt that she might have to kill him and take that leap through the window herself, even if it killed her as well. Otherwise, he would never relent with his obsession with replacing his dead wife with her.

She sat up in the bed and shivered, looking to the lower window pane for any sign of Gordon or Ian. When the window offered nothing but the view of the lamp lit street, she cried. She held her left hand in her right, massaging the place where Gordon's ring had been. She prayed that Gordon would not think that Charlotte's bones and April's jewelry meant that April was gone forever. Her hands shook and she wondered what had happened to the brave woman she had thought she had been. She could feel herself grinding her teeth and she swallowed her pain and grief and tried to think of a better future, not the twisted path to which Dreamville had brought her.

She listened to hear where Will might have gone in the house to travel through Dreamville. She tried to imagine where it might be. If the full lower pane in her bedroom acted as a transit, then Will probably was also using a window and most likely a large one for him to take Charlotte's body with him. She wiped the tears from her eyes and softly walked to the door to see if she were still a prisoner in the bedroom.

To her surprise, Will had forgotten to lock the door in his haste or perhaps, she thought, maybe he trusted her enough to allow her to leave the room. No matter, she thought. She was determined to go back to Burnock.

She undressed, tossing the coral silk nightgown in the corner. Whoever the Pamela Norris to whom it had belonged was, she was not her, was never her, and she wanted nothing to do with it. She thought of the different realities of Dreamville and the chart and how each choice led to a different path. She wondered what Will's Pamela

Norris had been like. What chance event had led that woman or girl to go into the direction that led her to a creature such as Will? She could not imagine anything ever placing herself in his arms - unless he was the one there in the most devastating event Dreamville had thrust upon her – the murder of her family and her rape.

Would that have driven her into Will's arms? Maybe the other Pamela, but not her she decided. It had to be some other insecurity, some other event or thing. Perhaps the other version of herself that Will had married had actually loved and felt comfortable with him. Maybe Will had been a different man before his wife had died. Maybe the loss of his wife was what drove him to madness.

As she dressed in her own original clothing she had worn when Will brought her here, she decided it did not matter what happened in the other timeline. He had said something about waiting 10 years for her. That meant that she would have just met Gordon when Will discovered her. That threw another kink in her timeline and then she realized that her timeline, that everyone's timeline was connected by those who came before and by those who came after. Perhaps Will's or Pamela's parents had married at a much younger age or maybe her mother in her life was not the mother of Will's wife. The infinite variations of time and space and dimensions that Dreamville presented was too much to consider.

Then she thought of something else. Why had Will not disrupted her friendship with Gordon when they were younger? Could he not act until she was then the same age as his wife? Were there laws of physics that she was unaware of? She laughed at that. So many questions, she thought. But she didn't care how any of it had come to be. She cared only about her family. Nothing else mattered. Could she murder Will? Did she have it within her end his existence? She didn't know. She just knew she had to go home.

Once she had finished dressing, she tiptoed to her bedroom door. She had to find Will now before he disappeared with Charlotte and find his key to the other times and places.

She crept down the steps, thankful that Will had placed a runner on the staircase that silenced her footsteps. When she reached the first floor rooms, she could not find him anywhere. The place where he had murdered Charlotte was scrubbed and smelled strongly of bleach and cleanser. There was no evidence upon her close examination of the room that Charlotte had died there.

She touched the doorframe and thought of how Charlotte had done everything she had for the same reason April was doing what she was doing – to find Gordon and retain his love once more. She wanted to feel sympathy for Charlotte, but she could not. Charlotte's sneering face came to her mind and she was glad that she had once less thing standing between her and her family. Charlotte be damned.

I have a son with Gordon, April thought. I have Ian. Charlotte had only had a brief affair with Gordon if she were to be believed. I had a life with Gordon. I had a family. Damn you, she wanted to scream and she hit the doorframe and cursed Charlotte for ever helping Will steal her happiness. She no longer felt remorse for how Will murdered Charlotte. All she felt was the anger that she knew she would need to help her find her way home.

Chapter Twenty

It was in the living room that she found Will climbing back through the shimmering front window that must have served as the doorway to where he had left Charlotte in Scotland. She thought of his words that they would find nothing but bones and April's jewelry and she saw that there was more to travelling through Dreamville that slipping through shimmering windows. And sadly, she realized that meant she would have to continue to play her pathetic role for Will until he trusted her enough to reveal how Dreamville worked, or at least how he moved through time and space.

His face flushed red when he saw April standing in the living room watching him climb through the liquid glass of the window. His clothing was filthy and blood stained. She knew he had been to Scotland as a certainty when she saw the thistle leaf tearing into the fabric of his navy blue blazer. There had existed in her mind that he had lied to her earlier in order to keep from trying to return, but the thistle was the clue she needed. So, she thought, he had taken Charlotte's body there to be found and mistaken for hers.

She feigned surprised and forced herself to rush to him, showing concern and touching his arm to guide him into the room.

"Will, are you alright? Where have you been? I became frightened being here alone."

He shook her arm off his and brushed the dirt from his clothing, trying to act as if what she had seen had been nothing. Instead of confiding in her, he turned his anger on her.

"You were not to leave your bedroom. Why are you dressed in those clothes? Were you trying to follow me?"

His anger was palpable and she feared that he would strike her.

She put on her best Pamela face and tried not to tear up, hoping that he would mistake her concern for him rather than fear of him.

"Will, please don't be angry. I didn't know what to wear. This is what I wore here. I just grabbed them and tried to dress and come find you. I swear I was only worried about you."

"Take them off."

April stepped back from him. She didn't know what to do.

"I said to take the fucking clothes off! Now!"

She crossed her arms against her chest protectively rather than folded in defiance of his orders. Her tears were not false now. They were real. All she could think of was being beaten or raped.

"Will, the window. People can see in from the street. Please let me go upstairs and change."

He went to the window pulled the drapes closed and then turned to her and began to tear at her blouse and jeans.

She raised her hand to him and held his hand firmly. For a brief second their eyes met and he saw that she would not fight him. He released her and stepped back to allow her room to undress. She unbuttoned the white blouse, removed it and then stepped out of the jeans as well as pulling the white canvas Keds from her feet.

He watched her closely as she undressed and then bent and grabbed the clothes and threw them in the fireplace where the flames engulfed them greedily. The rubber soles of Keds began to stink and he used the poker to pull them from the flames and put them in the ash bucket.

"The rest as well."

"Will, there's no need. I'll remove them upstairs."

"I said to take them off now. Don't make me hurt you."

She was mortified at being naked in front of him, but she had to do this to gain his trust. She held her breath and prayed that he would take this no further that he would not try to touch her. She removed her bra and bikini underpants and threw them into the fire herself.

He looked her over and then told her to turn around.

She did as he asked. She had never felt as shamed as she did now. Her hair was gone. Her clothing gone. Her wedding ring was on a rotting corpse somewhere in Scotland. She could not fight him in this condition. She started to place her arms across her breasts, but stopped. He had to believe that she was willing to accept becoming his Pamela.

"The curls in your hair will have to be straightened. We'll take you to a stylist and have it fixed. Why is there a scar on your side?"

She looked down. She had had her appendix removed three years ago in her real world. Obviously, his wife in Dreamville had had no such scar. She explained why the scar was there.

"We can have it surgically minimized. It's ugly. Pamela's body had no scars. Do you have any others?"

April shook her head.

"I don't think so. Maybe a few childhood scrapes from growing up with three brothers."

"Pamela had no brothers. Your body must be as pristine as hers was."

The words 'Pamela had no brothers' hurt her horribly and made her understand a little more about the woman Will had married. Three brothers had made April both tough and loved and protected. She could not imagine what Will's Pamela's life had been like without brothers.

For another five minutes, he examined her body closely. It was an excruciating time that seemed to drag on forever. Finally, he had seen everything he needed to see.

"Well, then. Go to your bedroom, put your nightgown

on and go back to bed. As for clothing, your clothing is where it always was."

"Will, I don't know where that is. I'm sorry. I'm just learning. Please don't be mad."

He nodded.

"Of course, of course. The evening has been stressful. I forgot. Just go through the walk-in closet and you'll find everything you need. Your toiletries are in the bathroom, but I suppose Charlotte had already shown you that. Now, good night."

April turned and wanted to run up the stairs, but walked as normally as she could considering she was naked. She had been terrified that he would rape her and she thanked God that he had done nothing more than burn her clothing. In the darkness at the top of the staircase, she looked back down into the living room and saw him still standing in the same place, transfixed by the flames that had burnt her clothing.

If he wanted his wife back so desperately, why had he not taken her, she asked herself, knowing that something was not right with him. Another question then bloomed in her mind. Why hadn't he gone back to the day he lost his Pamela and stopped her murder instead of spending ten years waiting for April?

It must be his madness that stopped him from seeing the possibilities that Dreamville had presented him. Surely he could see that he could have his own wife back rather than ripping April from her life. Insanity. It was all insanity. And if she didn't escape here soon, Dreamville would make her insane as well.

She quickly went into the bedroom, being sure to take the key from the outside lock so that she could lock herself into the bedroom, though deep inside herself she doubted that any lock could keep him from her if that was what he really wanted.

After putting the coral nightgown back on she went to the walk-in closet that Charlotte had previously guarded. Charlotte had kept it locked and had always placed her fresh clothing in the bathroom each morning before she showered.

April looked at the key and wondered if the key also fit the closet door. She tried to insert it and found it was much bigger that the lock on the closet. She looked around the room and found a hairpin that had fallen from her hair before Charlotte had cut her long hair off.

After almost 30 minutes she was no closer to opening

the locked door when she decided she would take the chance of facing Will again. She had no choice unless she wanted to spend the rest of her life in the sheer silk and lace night gown. She unlocked the door, took a deep breath and walked back down the stairs.

Will was still standing in the living room, but was looking out the window, although he was not seeing the street outside. Instead, the glass shimmered and he watched as a funeral was taking place at Burnock. She saw her family there and Sheila holding young Ian as Gordon knelt and placed a rose on a new grave.

Her gasp when she saw her name on the stone in front of Gordon brought Will from his fugue and just as she was about to leap through the window, he grabbed her by the waist and held her away from the shimmering vision until the window darkened and reflected their forms and the fire lit room behind them.

"Thank heavens that's over. Now we can move on with our lives."

She crumpled to the floor and wept. She had been inches away from her home and family. Her baby was so much older than when she had been stolen from him and Gordon looked ten years older. Her mouth opened in a silent wail and she reached out and touched the cold glass of the window. The pain that tore through her heart was without words. It felt as if her life was over. Gordon and her family thought her dead.

She laid in the floor staring at the blackened glass and tried to memorize everything she had seen in the vision of her world. It took a long time before she could move, but finally she stood and began to slap at Will, cursing him for stealing her life from her.

He pushed her roughly away from him as if she disgusted him by her inability to control her emotional response to what she had seen. He walked over to the fireplace and poked at the fire.

"I didn't steal your life. You caused all this when you went to your parents on our third anniversary and was murdered in a home invasion. That window, that window was the only thing that kept me sane when I saw you standing next to Gordon in another room. From that moment, I spent the next ten years trying to determine how to get you back here."

"You have no right to talk about what is fair and what is not. If you hadn't gone to your parents' home, you would have lived here, happy with me."

He ignored her and walked to the sofa to sit next to the fire. April tried to compose herself. He had just revealed a great deal about how he moved from place to place and she had to force herself to talk to him to find out more. No matter how she hated him, she knew she had to try to talk to him.

For a brief moment she looked at the discarded poker and thought of beating him with it, crushing his skull until there was nothing left of his hated face. But she pulled her grief inside herself and forced herself to take just a bit more time in ridding herself of him. If she were to act precipitously and he managed to escape, she might never be able to go home again.

"Will, I am not that Pamela. That Pamela existed in another place, another dimension or universe, whatever you want to call it. When you started travelling, you disrupted my life's path and my family's path. I don't know how it works, but that place, that Scotland, is where I belong."

He took a deep breath and sighed.

"Nonsense. From the moment I saw you in the window with that boy, I knew that you were not dead. I don't know what you're talking about – different dimensions or universes. You're being an idiot. Now, go to bed. I'm tired and bored with your constant nagging. Leave. Now."

April stood and looked at the window again and saw only the glass as it should be. She walked away from Will, knowing that he was completely mad, but she still had to learn from him how to get home. She forgot about the clothes closet, locked herself in the bedroom and cried herself to sleep, holding tightly to her heart the memory of seeing her family at her own funeral.

Chapter Twenty-One

As Gordon placed the rose on April's grave, he saw in the distance from the corner of his eye his wife in a coral gown, her hair cut short as she struggled to escape Will's grasp to get to them.

He seared the memory of her fight in his memory and closed his eyes, trying not to roar aloud over his frustration that he could not help her return. The vision had been so brief that even had he reached where she fought to come back, she would have vanished by the time he reached her.

But he was not the only one who saw her. Ian screamed louder than he had since Will had taken April from them. The tiny boy said the only word he had said since his birth – Momma. Everyone but Sheila and Gordon turned to witness his outburst. Gordon, because he had seen April first, and Sheila, who had seen April vanish just as Ian screamed for his momma. She stared at where April had appeared.

Gordon walked to Sheila and knew that she, too, had seen April. He took Ian in his arms and nodded to Sheila, a silent acknowledgement that they would talk later about what had just occurred. Ian lay his head of dark black curls against the shoulder of his father's charcoal suit, his heather blue gray eyes identical to those of his father. He grabbed the lapel of his father's coat and buried his face in the soft wool. Gordon could feel his tiny body shaking as he said Momma over and over so softly that no one but Gordon could hear him.

Gordon's mother, Claire, walked over to them and took her son's free arm and led her son and grandson back toward the house as the rest of the funeral party followed. Only April's mother remained at the grave. April's father moved to lead her with the rest of the family, but her mother looked at her husband.

"What happened? Two children in one year. First David and now April. Why? Why?"

She almost collapsed into her husband's arms and April's father nodded at Rick to help him. Rick left Lisa, now pregnant with the child that Gordon knew would be called David, and assisted his father. The grief that everyone there felt could not be denied, but for April's mother, the loss of two of her children was more than she could bear.

She spoke little during the afternoon and sat in the chair that April had sat in the afternoon before Alex's funeral, staring out at the grounds of Burnock and searching for a reason to live. She knew the saying that parents should never outlive their children, but she had never truly understood it until this year. It was Lisa who pulled her from the depths. Lisa sat down on a small stool before her and took her hands in her own.

"We weren't sure until this week and then . . . then, well, Rick and I wanted you to know that the baby is a boy, that we've chosen David as his name, if it's alright with you."

April's mother leaned forward and clasped Lisa to her chest.

"Yes, yes, that would be good. David will be remembered . . . and April, April gave us Ian. They had short lives, but they will always be with us."

Gordon had surrendered Ian to his grandmother

Claire and watched the scene with Lisa and April's mother play out across the room. He didn't have to hear them to know what was being said. The curse of Dreamville. And maybe the only comfort of Dreamville.

That afternoon he drank and he drank a great deal. The scotch seemed to fuel the anger he needed to make things right, to bring April home, to even reset this life so that maybe even David would not die in that horrible accident. But most of all, he needed to make Will and Charlotte pay, to stop them from ever hurting him, his family or April's family.

He thought of her screaming and reaching out to them as Will held her back. She looked so little like his wife and instead like April made to look like someone else. There was something he was missing, something about Will's persistent drive to attain April. Just as he tried to think of how he might go about finding out, he was approached by Sean. Before Sean could speak, he pulled him away from the others in the room.

"Sean, could you see if there was a man named Jonathan Williams who lost his wife in Connecticut about ten years ago? It might be important."

Sean was flummoxed by Gordon's request. What the

hell did a man named Jonathan Williams have to do with April's death? It was then that his policeman's gut kicked in and he wondered if Gordon knew something he had not mentioned before.

"Yes, Gordon, I suppose I could. Why?"

Gordon couldn't explain to Sean the reason why, but the idea that Gordon and April had existed in both Connecticut and Scotland at the same time made him wonder if the man he had always known as Will was also the man in America known as Jonathan Williams. Could this Jonathan Williams, the one involved in April's quilt show be the key to solving the quest that Dreamville had put before him? Maybe, just maybe, if he could just solve this riddle, he could get April back.

"Another thing, Sean. Was a DNA analysis ever done on the remains?"

Sean stepped back in shock. Gordon hadn't seen the body or rather what was left of it, but April's things were there, including her wedding band.

"Gordon, you've got to accept . . ."

"No, I want the DNA analysis done. I'll pay for the damned thing. Please, just have it done."

The desperation in Gordon's eyes convinced Sean

that Gordon would not let this go.

"I'll see to it, Gordon, but wait until the family has returned home. Now is not the right time."

Gordon grasped Sean's arm tightly.

"But you'll check on the other thing as soon as possible, the Jonathan Williams thing. And see if there was an art show in Manhattan in December of last year, a show of art quilts at a place called the Nora Epstein Gallery."

Sean had no idea where Gordon was pulling this information from, but as his oldest friend, he would do it for him. Sean truly believed that it was April in that grave and dreaded what he would have to do. Perhaps this would finally convince Gordon of the same thing.

"Yes, Gordon. First thing tomorrow. But tonight, tonight you need to be with your family," he said and walked into the room to speak with other mourners.

Gordon reached out and touched the window pane.

I will find you my love, I promise, he thought, echoing his thoughts of his past visit to a future version of Dreamville.

Chapter Twenty-Two

The next morning Sean reached out to a friend he had at Interpol and called New Haven, Connecticut to see if a man named Jonathan Williams was a resident. He also did an internet search on the Nora Epstein Gallery and was surprised to find it as well as contact information on the gallery and the location of it.

But the thing that stunned him was that there was a man named Jonathan Williams who had moved there ten years ago and had only recently left the area. His current residence was unknown. Sean thanked his friend and leaned back in his chair and stared out the window of his office at the main street of the village, now empty of tourists and residents. The January weather had even driven the locals indoors.

He picked up his phone and started to punch in the number for the Nora Epstein Gallery. He was hesitant to make this call as he no idea what possible connection she might have to April Stewart. When the call was answered he had expected to speak with an employee, but Nora Epstein herself answered the telephone.

He briefly explained who he was and a short statement that he was investigating a crime that involved a local family.

"I know this may sound strange, but do you know either a Jonathan Williams or a woman named April Stewart?"

He could hear Nora's sharp intake of breath even across the bad transatlantic connection.

"Yes, I know Williams. He owes me quite a bit of money for an art piece that he never paid for. Luckily, the show was a success and I eventually found another buyer for the piece."

"I see. But what about April Stewart? Do you know anyone by that name?"

Nora hesitated and Sean impatiently waited for her memory to give him either a yes or no answer.

"April . . . Stewart? Are you sure the last name was

Stewart?"

"Well, she was named Norris before she married Gordon Stewart here in Scotland. She was American and she moved here about two years ago."

"April Norris?" Nora asked. "Of course, I knew April Norris. It was her show that Williams caused the problems for me. She was a quilt artist, mixed media you know, and her show, Pieces of April, was a smashing success. She went into labor at the show and was hustled away by her family. Unfortunately, I never saw her again after that."

"It was the strangest thing. I visited her mother's shop once before the show, but when I went back to pay April, the shop was closed. Empty. And no one in that little town would even talk to me about how to find the Norris family."

Pieces started to click together in Sean's head, but the part about April being in Manhattan the year before Ian's birth made no sense. And why had her family never mentioned anything about this? He could see that the closing of the shop probably occurred around the time April's brother had died after April had disappeared last January. But the rest of it made no sense. He was trying to make connections when he heard Nora's voice on the telephone.

"Hello, are you still there?"

"Yes, Ms. Epstein, I'm sorry. What did you say?"

"I said that if April Norris became April Stewart could you inform her that I'm holding her funds from her show for her. It was a very, very successful show. She made quite a bit of money."

Sean paused and wiped his eyes, trying to imagine how any of this could be explained.

"Ms. Epstein, I doubt that the two women could be the same as April Stewart was here last year. In fact, she disappeared and her . . . remains were just recently found near Edinburgh. But if I come across an April Norris, I'll be sure to get in touch with you.

"Well, if there was foul play with April Norris, I would bet good money that Jonathan Williams had something to do with it.

Sean sat forward and leaned against his desk, finishing his notes on what he had discovered today and trying to get off the call with Epstein.

"Well, Ms. Epstein, if you hear from either of them, please ring me up," Sean said and concluded the phone call by giving Nora his telephone number, including his mobile number.

Gordon was surprised when several hours later Sean appeared at the door of Burnock and pushed his way past Gordon.

"You have some explanations to provide, Gordon. Now."

Sean was determined to know exactly how Gordon had known what took him an entire day to discover and now he, as Gordon had said, seriously doubted that Pamela April Norris Stewart's remains were in the churchyard.

"Sean, the family is still here and about to dine. I can't talk about it now, but I can later. Join us for dinner. We'll talk after everyone's retired for the evening."

Sean nodded his head and followed Gordon into the dining hall which was full. Sean noticed the furtive glances that passed between Sheila and Gordon and decided that Sheila might be included in their little conversation later.

He tried not to show his anger that important information had been kept from him, but he did and spent a pleasant, though tense, evening with Gordon's family. Only small Ian seemed to keep the sadness away from the family. A child who had not spoken until his mother's funeral seemed to know everyone's name quite well. It was as if the tiny boy knew that something was about to change and that he was preparing for it.

Sean shook his head and spoke with everyone about only trivial matters. Sean watched them each closely and knew one thing as a certainty – that if the body in the churchyard was not April, all their heartbreak would begin anew.

Chapter Twenty-Three

Gordon had no idea how to explain Dreamville to Sean. He had enlisted the help of both Sheila and Andrew for this late night discussion and he was unsure that even they would be able to completely help him explain the real events of the last ten years.

After everyone had retired for the evening, Gordon sat down with Sean, Sheila, and Andrew. He felt as if he were reliving the same night he had had to try to explain the events to Andrew. He remembered how calm April had been that night. She had stopped the arguments, the confusion, the anger and sadness by simply leading him from the room and to their bed. His chest constricted at the thought of that time with her, that precious, beautiful and brief time before it all went wrong.

But April was not here to help him now. He only had Sheila and Andrew to help explain the madness of their life. Could Sean possibly comprehend what his life had been like, much less the idea of what April always called Dreamville? Could he convince Sean that he was not insane as his family had thought for ten years? How could Sean understand what he and April had never been able to truly comprehend?

He looked across the table at Sean and pulled at his hair, not even knowing how to start such a tale that seemed one told by a madman or a murderer.

It was Sheila who saw his anguish and who came to his rescue. Slowly, but surely, she related the story of Dreamville. At times, Sean would stare alternately in shock and horror at the three of them, but he never interrupted Sheila's narrative.

By the time she finished her tale, Sean's face was completely drained of color and for a moment Gordon thought that he would faint. Other worlds, other dimensions or universes, people able to cause people to hurt themselves but not others. It was all too fantastical for anyone to believe and Sean would have accused them of April's murder then and there had he not seen for himself the truth and grief in all their faces.

"I'm still not sure how this 'Dreamville' idea works," Sean said. "I know that there are many things that we do not know about the universe, that our intelligence is that of an ant compared to what we do not know, but the three of you must see that no rational, logical person could ever accept what you have told me."

Gordon sighed and bent his head. It was hopeless and he should never have brought Sean into this. Surprisingly, it was Andrew who spoke up to rebuke Sean for his words.

"I felt just as you did when Alex died last year, when I walked from the hallway at Burnock into a bedroom in a Kensington house only to find my wife and April bound and lying upon the floor, when I saw that *creature* and then find us all back in Gordon's bedroom here."

"But I've learned in the past year or so that there is so much I will never know. I can only know that I love my family as Gordon loves his. I'll never understand Dreamville, but I do believe that somehow, someway it exists, if nothing else other than something our brains cannot comprehend."

Sean stood and began to pace around the room, at times shaking his head and then nodding his head, as if he were arguing with himself over the discoveries of the day. He finally returned to his seat and then he began to inform the others of his own weird discoveries of the day through his contacts and conversations with others.

"Then she could still be alive!" Sheila exclaimed and wiped tears from her cheek.

"Somehow we might be able to get her away from Will. When we saw her yesterday in the churchyard, she was trying to escape from Will. I could see the pain and struggle in her face and Ian certainly saw her - a child who has never spoken till that afternoon."

Gordon drained a second glass of scotch and felt the pain in his chest again. He tried to stand and suddenly he felt the room begin to spin.

This is odd, he thought, as he fell onto the floor unconscious.

He was just as surprised to find his father standing over him where he was lying on the sofa.

"What happened? Did something happen. Is April here?"

His father, who had not been privy to their conversation earlier, assumed it was his grief that produced his question.

"Gordon, son. No. Remember. You have not taken care of yourself. You have not been eating and you've been drinking quite a bit. I did a check on your blood sugar and it was quite high. I need you to see another doctor and have your blood levels checked. I'm afraid you may have inherited your grandfather's type II diabetes, but I can't properly make the diagnosis. Another doctor will have to do that."

He stood and placed his instruments in a small leather bag and tried to hide the fear on his face. Finally he turned to face Gordon.

"I'm sorry, son. You did not need this after everything you've suffered. I'll call Dr. Watt in the morning and make arrangements for you to see him."

At that point, Sheila came into the room with a tray laden with a sandwich and a large glass of milk.

"Eat that and then go to bed. Enough late nights. You have a son who depends on you. You cannot allow him to suffer no matter how much you grieve," his father said and left the room.

Gordon sat up and stared at Sean, Sheila and Andrew.

"Well, bloody hell, why am I not surprised? I was diabetic in the future Dreamville. I should have seen this coming," he said as he took a large bite of the sandwich.

"What future Dreamville, Gordon? You've never talked about that," Sheila asked.

He realized he had said too much and inadvertently looked at Andrew whose face flushed bright red. Sheila was not one not to notice her husband's reaction and she became angry, thinking that Gordon had shared something with Andrew that she did not know.

Andrew sat down on the arm of the chair next to her, but looked at Gordon.

"You know. How do you know?"

Gordon drank deeply of the glass of milk to keep from responding to Andrew's question with a lie, but before he could speak, Sheila grabbed her husband's arm tightly.

"I seem to have developed a heart condition," Andrew said and pulled a tiny vial of nitroglycerin from his jacket pocket.

"I had a small event last fall. This was the best they could offer."

"But why didn't you tell me? And surely there's some sort of surgical procedure that can help. A bottle of pills can't be the only answer."

Andrew hugged Sheila against his chest and led her

from the room. It reminded Gordon again of the night April had led him away. He was not going to tell Andrew what he knew of the future. He grieved for his cousin's future loss, but hoped that it would not occur for many years.

Sean had watched the entire scene without comment and now stared at Gordon as if he were a mystical, perhaps, magical man.

"He's going to die?"

Gordon nodded, but could not look Sean in the eye.

"So you traveled to Dreamville in the future and that's how you knew the things you told me."

This time Gordon shook his head.

"No, after the Dreamville alternative, I found myself back in Manhattan with April, in a version where I had never taken her to Burnock and where Alex still lived."

He wiped his mouth and put the cloth napkin over the remains of the sandwich. He had eaten as much as he could force himself to eat.

Now he looked Sean straight in the eye and related the events of the year leading up to Ian's birth and April's capture.

"Wait, how could you be both places? I saw you both

here. We spent many evenings together in this room. You could not have been in New York," Sean said.

Gordon shrugged his shoulders.

"April and I had no idea that we were here as well until Dreamville flipped a switch and we found ourselves upstairs with her giving birth. And here's the kicker – our families know nothing of the year in Manhattan or Jonathan Williams or that art show. To them, this reality is the only one that as ever existed."

"And yet, as you discovered today, there is a woman in New York by the name of Nora who remembers everything as it happened there, including her hatred for Williams, who, I suppose, is and always has been the nightmare Will who has tortured my life for the past decade."

Gordon leaned back into the sofa and momentarily closed his eyes.

"Sean, I believe I need to follow my father's instructions and try to rest. No matter what else happens I have to keep going for Ian."

Sean gave him a small wry smile and shook hands goodbye.

"You know, Gordon, I'd arrested anyone else who

had told me such a story. Why I believe you makes no sense, but I do."

Chapter Twenty-Four

Just as Gordon had known, his visit with Doctor Watt proved him to have type II diabetes. The doctor told him that if Gordon were careful that the disease could be managed with diet, exercise, and pills. He was not at the point where he would need insulin yet and the doctor told him he might never.

Gordon smiled and thanked him and walked away from the office knowing that the insulin needles were just years away. He got into his Aston Martin and proceeded home thinking of April and how much he and Ian needed her now.

For a fleeting second, he thought of veering the car off the Highland road, the silver rims of the wheels spinning wildly to gain traction on empty air before the car flew downward onto the craggy rocks. The thought crossed his mind for less than a millisecond when Ian and April's faces filled his mind. The steering wheel stayed firm in his hands and he knew that he had to live, no matter how much he hurt or he would never be able to bring April back to her son and if nothing else mattered, that one thing did.

Both his and April's family were waiting in the parlor when he returned. He walked into the room, tossed his keys into a brass dish and smiled at his new, extended family.

April's mother was holding Ian on her lap as he tried to disassemble his own ring of large and brightly colored keys. When he saw Gordon, he dropped the keys and raised his arms for his father who took him and held him closely, kissing the little curls that had replaced his early baby hair.

Gordon winced and looked away for a moment. There was so much April was missing. He tried to think of what to say but could only hold his small son.

"I have grandfather's disease," he said, "But I need not suffer grandfather's demise, not if I take care of myself, you know – proper diet and all that."

He thought his mother was about to cry, but his father began to talk about all the ways of managing the disease and how he should return to America with both families, bringing young Ian there as well.

"Father, please. I know you mean well, but I cannot leave here. Ian will thrive here and my medical care will be just as good as if I were in Manhattan."

He handed Ian back to April's mother and Ian wrapped his little arms around his grandmother's neck, lying his head against her shoulder and blinking his eyes closed to succumb to the easy sleep that only the very young could fall into.

"I know that you all want to see Ian more and I will make every attempt to make that happen, but I will not leave Burnock. This was my home with . . . this is my home and I'll not leave it."

The discussion went on for almost an hour with everyone but Sheila and Andrew urging him to return to America. They understood why he would never leave Burnock. They knew that he would spend the rest of his life there if necessary waiting for April to return.

When Mrs. MacCurdy announced that dinner was ready, they all moved into the dining hall and began to finally talk of their own plans to return to America, relieving Gordon of the need to continue to try to convince them that he would not change his mind.

That night he dreamed of April again and could feel her warm body next to his, yet when he tried to call her name and pull himself from the dream, he felt as if he were shouting with no sounds coming from his mouth. When he awoke and finally forced her name from his throat in an almost soundless rasp, he found the bed empty as always. He moved his hands across the sheets where her body should have been and the cold linens seemed like a cold joke at his need for her.

It was always then, in the darkest part of the night that he sometimes contemplated a life without her and that seemed a life unimaginable. There were times that he wished that he could stop the dreams where she was next to him in bed, but he then cursed himself for ever forgetting the place of her body next to her.

Those nights he would know that he would have to learn to love what he did have – his small son he had delivered from April in the bed he slept. He again cursed anything that would stop him from dreaming of her.

His restlessness always seemed timed to Ian's. In the

dark, he could hear his son almost talking, babbling in the weird language that only babies could speak and understand. One time he heard Ian say "Momma" and he jumped from the bed to find Ian smiling at the window.

He moved to the rocker next to the crib and began to doze off. His was back to the window and he did not know that Ian could see his mother in the window panes, nor that the windows, just as all the places April had placed in her quilts, were doorways to where she was now.

So, he slept in the rocker and his son stared at April, knowing that she was just a movement away through the panes of the window glass.

It would be another week before Gordon made the connection between April's quilts and the places around Burnock.

A week later after his receipt of his diagnosis of diabetes, Gordon and Ian waved good-bye to his family. April's mother had taken it the hardest and fought leaving longer than anyone else. Had it not been for Rick and Lisa's presence, she might have completely broken down. But every time she began to mourn the losses of David and April, Lisa and Rick would help her by giving her a future that held more than death and lost children.

But finally Gordon had them all bundled into cars and heading out from Burnock, leaving him alone there with Ian and his few household servants.

They were barely out of sight of the house when he quickly walked into the house and picked up the telephone receiver to call Sean. He had to know. He would not believe those were really April's bones in that grave until forensic science told him they were. He knew they could not be. He had seen her struggling to escape from Will that day. She had to be alive somewhere in Dreamville and the exhumation of her body was the only way to prove she lived.

"They're gone. Bring the crew and come now. I have to know as soon as possible."

"Gordon, it will take more than a few weeks to do the DNA study in Edinburgh. I know that seems impossibly long to you, but I can't make things move any faster."

"Well, I can. Send the sample to a private lab where I won't have to wait more than a few days. I'll pay for whatever it costs."

"Gordon . . ."

"Sean, I canna wait. I have to find her. For Ian. He has to have a mother. Sean, I need her. Please do this for me. Whoever Jonathan Williams is or wherever he is, he has April. I know she's alive."

He heard Sean rattling papers around before Sean responded.

"We're on our way, Gordon. God forgive us all if it is April in that grave. Her final resting place should not be disturbed."

Gordon started to speak, but Sean stopped him.

"I know what you think. Just leave it to me now. I'll call you as soon as I know. And do not come out to the churchyard. I don't want to see you anywhere nearby, not Sheila or Andrew either.

"They left for Edinburgh this morning. Everyone has left. It's just myself and Ian. We'll be out of your way."

"And Sean, thank you. No one knows what this has been like but you and Sheila and Andrew. So, thank you. Thank you for believing me."

After he hung up the telephone he took Ian's hand in his.

"How would you like to visit the burn, young lad? I'll show you where I'll teach you to fish one day. Come let's go dress for this blustery day."

Gordon had no idea that he was about to discover one

of the first doors to April's location.

Chapter Twenty-Five

In Dreamville, April sat in the dark bedroom each night waiting to see her infant son. Will never seemed to include her in any activities except for supper. The rest of the time she spent in the bedroom, alone and sad. Will went out most evenings and unknown to him he left her to stare at the single lower window pane in her bedroom, praying that it might be a night when she could see Ian or even Gordon.

Ian always saw her and she could tell by his happy gurgles that he was trying to talk to her, but Gordon had not seen her and she could see into the room through the glass as he wrenched about in the bed. She heard him call her name on more than one occasion.

Her body ached for him, for his touch, for his strong

arms holding her as she slept. Some nights she wept in frustration and young Ian, seeing her sadness, would begin to wail, too. She would then try to soothe him, but no matter how often she touched the glass, it was an impermeable barrier between them. She could not understand why the window downstairs seemed to be a way home, but this window just a view into her real world. She thought perhaps that maybe the size of the glass made the difference on the Burnock side. The panes of glass in the window at Burnock were small and ancient rondels. She might be able to fly through the bedroom window in Will's house. It was a large enough piece of glass that she could fit through, but if it only connected to the yellow bedroom window, then she thought she might have no chance of making it through alive. The smaller panes might cut her into pieces.

But she knew that there had to be other doors or windows between this Dreamville and Burnock and she realized the connection of the quilts long before Gordon did simply because she had seen Will emerge from the downstairs picture window and she had seen the family chapel and the cemetery there. That window obviously represented the Chapel Quilt just as window in her bedroom reflected the yellow bedroom quilt

That accounted for two of the quilts she had made of places in Burnock. She tried to recall the quilts and remembered each one. There were the burn and sea quilts, of course, but the water could be as dangerous as the window panes in the yellow bedroom. The bench could be a possibility as well as the trestle table in the kitchen, but the auld moon and the thistle made no sense other than perhaps a place in one of the pastures. As for the claw foot tub quilt, she could not think of what it represented other than the tender moments she had spent with Gordon in that tub. The Arch quilt and The Bench seemed the most likely places and probably the safest, but where would she find the corresponding places in Will's house, if all ten of them existed there. The churchyard had not appeared in the window since the funeral and Will had shuttered the large window and locked it to keep her from attempting to move through it if it had opened to her again.

She decided one night as she watched Gordon struggling in his sleep that she would spend every moment that Will was not there looking for the other transits from Dreamville to Burnock. She wondered if transits between the worlds of Dreamville and other realities were everywhere, but that most people never saw them and could not imagine they existed; but, then she thought most people had never been through what she and Gordon had experienced. Had it not been for Gordon and Ian, she knew she would have lost her mind trying to understand why the doorways to different realities, roads not taken as Frost as said, were open to her and not everyone.

And that, she realized might be Will's weakness. He thought that by making Gordon think she was dead that he would kill her desire to return home. He obviously had not seen the unending diversity of what Dreamville represented. He only saw the openings into her one world. His obsession with Pamela, with possessing a substitute for his dead wife made him blind to the unending universes and dimensions that were offered.

April believed that Will had never loved anyone as she loved Gordon and that he had definitely underestimated a mother's will when it came to being with her child.

That error on his part would prove his undoing. He would never understand that she would never give up trying to return home, whether he had fooled Gordon or not with Charlotte's bones wearing April's jewelry. Somehow April knew that Gordon had not given up on her either. She watched the sun rising in Burnock through the window pane and saw both her loves finally asleep as the window pane darkened once more to the street outside Will's house.

Tomorrow night. Tomorrow night she would begin to search the house for the other transits from Dreamville to her home. Good god, she thought, what had inspired her to make those quilts except some subconscious warning that she would need to make them to find her way home? And she was going to find them and she was going home. Not Will, not shuttered windows or dangerous water such as the burn or the sea would stop her from getting to her husband and child.

Only someone who had loved so deeply and strongly could understand her unyielding refusal to never let them go, to never give them up, even if it cost her life in getting there.

She heard Will coming in the front door and climbing the staircase just as she was moving evidence of her nightly vigil from his view should he ever enter the room. Tonight she heard him pause outside her bedroom and she was terrified that tonight was the night he had chosen for them to "resume" their marital relationship. She held her breath until she finally heard him go down the hallway to his own room.

She said a small prayer of thanks and exhaled a great rush of air in relief. She could not stand the thought of his touching her, but if it somehow helped her return home to Burnock, then she knew she might have to take on his sexual advances. Anything, even that, if necessary. She would do anything to leave Dreamville.

Chapter Twenty-Six

Gordon carried Ian on his shoulders across the pasture behind Burnock to where the burn flowed down from the Highland snow.

The boy bounced on his father's shoulders and his giggles sounded like the sound of the water running around the rocks of the burn. Ian pounded his tiny hands against his father's head, the thick Scottish wool mittens and cap protected both his hands and his head from the cold winter weather.

Once they were close enough for Ian to see the burn without any danger of the rushing water, Gordon lifted him down and held him in his arms.

Gordon glanced around and thought that this was probably where Alex had brought April when they rode here that morning. He suddenly shivered, not for the cold, but from some unknown source and he felt as if he were being warned. And that was the second that young Ian wriggled from his arms and waddled toward the burn screaming for his Momma.

The tiny boy moved surprisingly fast and Gordon had barely caught his tweed coat before Ian fell headlong into the water.

"Ian! No! No!" He could not understand how the child had escaped from him so quickly until in a small pool that was eddying around a large stone that he saw April's face. Her head was bowed and she was sitting in a strange room with Will sitting across from her.

Gordon could not hear what Will was saying to her, but she looked and acted nothing like his April. She wore strange, conservative dress and her long, beautiful dark curls were gone. Her hair was almost flat against her head and she looked as if she had lost weight.

He realized that the angle of the view of her in the room was more than just looking down into the burn. It was as if he was in the room with them but high above them, as if almost looking from the ceiling. He tilted his head and struggled to see her more closely without falling into the burn.

Suddenly Will stood and walked across the room and touched her cheek. Gordon saw the almost imperceptible wince that flashed across April's face when Will touched her cheek before she gave a small smile and nodded at Will. Then Will left the room and this time Gordon could hear the distinct slam of a door.

It was then and only then that Ian called "Momma" and to Gordon's shock, April walked closer to them and looked up as if she were looking through a window or something high.

"Gordon, my Scotsman, you haven't given up, have you?"

Gordon was so stunned to hear her voice that he began to stammer until Ian began to clap his hands at the sight and sound of his mother.

"Am I mad? April, how can this be? Is that you? God, I have lost my mind. I'm talking to my dead wife in in a pool in the burn."

"Oh, Gordon, you're not mad and I am not dead. You know that. It is me. It truly is. God, I've missed you both so much and Ian . . ." she sniffed back her tears. "Ian has grown so much. I've missed so much. I should never have gone with this insane man."

Gordon looked around to see if anyone else was within hearing range before he looked into the burn and spoke to April.

"What can I do, April? I somehow knew it was not you we buried that day. I saw you that day for this first time in almost a year. You were fighting Will. Oh god, April, how can I bring you home?"

April turned at a sound that only she heard and lowered her voice.

"I can't talk long, love. The quilts. Remember the quilts. They're the doors back to you."

She whirled around and looked out into the room again and then turned back to Gordon and Ian.

"He's coming back. You've got to get away Ian away from the burn in case Will hears him. He'll throw the mirror away and I'll have one less way to come home. I love you both. Remember the quilts, Gordon. The quilts."

And just as quickly as she was there, she was gone and the water turned dark and reflected the leafless woods and gray stones around where Gordon and Ian stood.

Ian flung himself against his father's shoulder and began to cry for his momma again and this time Gordon almost joined him in his anguished tears.

What had she said? He had to remember it all. He had to rush back to his study at Burnock and write it all down before he forgot. He began to run from the burn and through the back pasture, clasping the still weeping Ian to his chest.

Sean, who was still working with the others on the exhumation, saw Gordon running toward the house just as the workmen began to raise the coffin from the ground. He began to hurriedly walk to Gordon to stop his progress, mistakenly thinking that Gordon was headed for the grisly scene taking place in the graveyard.

"Gordon, you promised. Leave now and for God's sake get your son away from here!"

Gordon was gasping for breath and pushed past Sean and ran into the house with Sean following closely behind him.

"Mrs. MacCurdy! Mrs. MacCurdy!" Gordon cried out and the older woman came from the back of the house.

"Take Ian upstairs for his nap. He may be cold, so make sure he gets warmed up."

The woman took the child without a question and began to walk up the staircase as Gordon ran back through the Great Hall, through the parlor and into his study, still followed by Sean, who continued to object to Gordon's presence in the house.

"Gordon, talk to me! You promised not to return until after we had finished and you run back here with April's son there to see . . . oh God, I hope he didn't see anything."

Gordon was still ignoring Sean and had taken paper from his desk drawer and was writing as quickly as he could.

Sean's patience finally gave out and he slammed his fist against the wooden desk.

For the first time, Gordon looked up at him as he had only then realized that Sean had been talking to him since he ran back to Burnock.

"What the bloody hell are you doing, Gordon? What's so much more important than what's happening outside?"

Gordon suddenly remembered that the exhumation was taking place, but then he remembered April's words to him from the burn and he began write again.

Sean sat down in the chair next to the fireplace and waited. Sooner or later Gordon would have to answer him.

"Gordon, you do realize that we're exhuming April's

body for DNA testing out there don't you?"

Gordon did not pause in his writing or even look up at Sean, but he did respond.

"That is not April. I know now for sure. I saw her. I don't know who is in that grave, but it's not her. She's alive."

Sean stared at Gordon in horror, afraid that his old friend really was mentally ill.

"Gordon, you say you saw her. Where was she? Did she speak to you?"

Gordon did not answer at first. He completed writing everything April had told him and he looked at Sean.

In for a penny, in for a pound, he thought and leaned back into his desk chair. How to explain that his wife had spoken to him from an eddy in the burn? That might seal Sean's belief in his insanity forever, but he still told Sean everything and was not surprised by the increasing fear that was evident on his best friend's face.

Sean did not know what to say. He was speechless at what Gordon had just disclosed to him. The whole ideal of another world Gordon called "Dreamville" had been bad enough, but now Gordon was speaking to his dead wife in the burn at the back of the estate. How could he possibly respond to that?

"I know you think I've totally gone over the edge, Sean, but I haven't. I have no proof other than a child who can barely speak, but it is true. This Jonathan Williams has her and the quilts from the quilt show are the answer she said."

Gordon walked around the desk and began to pace in front of the fireplace near where Sean sat, still trying to decide what to say or do.

"Here's the thing. I only remember the one quilt – the one that I bought in the other world. I think it was called The Arch and it was a study of the arched gateway into the garden. There were red flowers in the garden that looked wet, but I think there was something she used to give it that effect. I remember small polished, cut stones used to simulate the path and that the fabric had been treated somehow to make it look as if it were the stone of the arch. That quilt I remember so clearly, but I've been through the arch here at Burnock and I've never seen her there."

He paused and stared out the study windows into the garden. He thought of the times he had seen April and realized suddenly that those times were times that they were both in the same place shown in her quilt, as if she had left pieces of herself in those quilts to give him clues as to where he could find her.

"Bloody hell! I can't remember the others, although I think the chapel and the burn were ones as well. I need you to call that Epstein woman in Manhattan and find out the other names of the quilts and what they looked like. Maybe that was what she meant when she told me to remember the quilts."

Sean watched as Gordon began to pace back and forth again. He began to wonder if he should contact Gordon's father. This had gone too far. He should never have agreed to the exhumation, but he had, and with Gordon's money they would know it was April in the graveyard in a few days. He decided to wait to call Gordon's father until after the DNA results came back. Until then, he would watch Gordon closely and try to stay at the estate as much as possible.

"Well, Gordon, we'll know about the DNA in a day or so. Let's just take it one step at a time until then," he said and placed his hand on Gordon's shoulder.

Gordon looked at Sean's hand on his shoulder and saw that the gesture was supposed to be calming, that Sean had not believed a word he had said.

"I don't have time to wait. I know it's not April. If you won't call the Epstein woman, I will. We have to know what the other quilts were called and what they looked like. That's the one thing April insisted on saying – 'Remember the quilts, Gordon.' I think she was trying to tell me that the quilts were the sites of how she could come back here or we could go there."

Sean shook his head and bowed his head. He wasn't very proud of himself right now. He had failed to protect his good friend from himself. He stood and walked to the desk and looked at the things that Gordon had written, Most of it made no sense. Only one line made a chill run through him.

Gordon had written, "Is Charlotte dead?"

Sean knew that Charlotte was the imaginary woman from London. What in the world had happened to his friend? Had his grief truly driven him mad?

Chapter Twenty-Seven

April had quietly run up the stairs as she heard one of the servants coming through the house. Although she wasn't sure if anyone other than she or Will could see through the ways into her world, she could not risk anyone seeing Gordon or Ian and reporting it to Will. She had to be very, very careful not to get caught looking for the ways home. After all, Will had made it quite clear to everyone in the household that she had spent the last years in a mental institution. Why would they ever believe the truth? If she were in their position, would she believe it?

Sadly, this one way out might be as impossible as the bedroom or the locked shutters. It was a large mirror hanging above the fireplace that seen to connect to the image in the burn quilt. It had certainly looked like the burn where Gordon and Ian had been standing.

She prayed that Gordon would understand the few things she had been able to tell him before she had to run away. Would he remember the quilts? She didn't even know if he had seen all of them at the show in Dreamville and if he had not, he might miss the one place where he could help her.

As she closed the door to her bedroom and walked to the chair by the window where she watched her baby, she thought of Dreamville. Why had she ever called it that? She had thought it was a product of her dreams or imagination. It took a long time, really not until she had seen that woman's family quilt, that she had seen that Dreamville was just as real as her world, that all the different places she had called Dreamville were just variations or branches of where she might have gone in life or where other versions of herself or the world had gone.

She thought of the world where Will's Pamela had existed and she shivered, unable to believe that any version of herself would have thought him right for her. But, she remembered the charming person he had been when she had been making the quilts. She could see that a lonely April might found his flattery and attention attractive.

Truthfully, she had found it that way after a while. He had worked hard and long to gain her trust, to make feel as if she were important at a time when she felt alone and miserable.

She could see how that Pamela would have succumbed to Will's charm. Without Gordon, without friends and family she would have had very little to live for. Will might have presented his Pamela with the only person who cared if she lived or died.

Loneliness was a terror that filled most people, she thought. It could drive people to make stupid mistakes, even cause them to end their lives. How could self-destruction be a selfish act if there was no one there, was never really anyone there? If Will's Pamela had been as lonely as she was now, she could understand why she had given up her life to those people so easily.

But April had a reason to live if she could escape this hell her life had become. She still had Gordon and Ian and a family who still lived and loved her.

Either way, none of what Will's Pamela had experienced mattered. She was not his April or Pamela or anyone who belonged in this world. She had to continue her search. The ten places into her world were here. She had no doubt of that now.

If Will had pulled Charlotte into his world or plan, it had to be from one version of Dreamville where she had either lost Gordon or been rejected by him, but April also did not think Charlotte and Will had been from the same version of Dreamville. She had been unwittingly, but willingly, pulled into his plan to replace Will's dead wife with April. Charlotte could not have seen the devious nature of Will and that was what led to her demise. Charlotte had wanted nothing but to return to her own version of Dreamville with Gordon and Will had found the perfect dupe in her.

April sat in the Windsor chair and lightly ran her fingers along the edge of the arm, letting her mind wander for a few minutes, wondering if Pamela had ever sat in this chair and had seen another world through the window pane as April had. The glass of the window was spotless, which did not surprise April. Will was demanding of everyone and everything. She had once accidentally moved a footstool in the living room and he had angrily put in back in place, glaring at her as if to silently put her in place as well.

She rarely touched anything in the house after that

except during her evening forays searching for her door home. And, even then, she had taken great care to place everything back to its original position, even carrying a small cloth with her lest she leave even the slightest smudge or fingerprint as evidence of her presence.

Several hours passed and the light in the street was beginning to wash everything in a yellow, dusky glow when she heard Will's return. She supposed that she should return downstairs. He had said that she was to be waiting for his return, but his level of civility or cruelty often told her of her mistakes.

As she passed by the peer mirror in her bedroom she saw a woman she barely recognized as herself. The haircut, the make-up, the conservative, almost prep school clothing made her look like a completely different woman. Also, by her countenance, a woman beaten down by this life, by Will, by this world she called Dreamville.

She sighed and went to greet the man who called himself her husband, but who had stolen her from her real husband and child. Tonight. Tonight she had to find the way home. She only prayed that Gordon was doing the same in their real world.

Chapter Twenty-Eight

Gordon knew, could see that Sean thought him mad. He didn't care as long as the road led him back to April. As April sat in her Windsor chair thinking of how to find a way home, Gordon sat in his desk chair in his study staring into the garden and remembering the spring morning he had watched her walking there with Alex. He thought of the woman he had seen reflected in the water of the burn and hoped that only her physical appearance had changed and not her fierce determination to live, to return to them.

It had been two days since the exhumation and Sean had yet to call with information on the DNA results. Gordon knew what the results would be and he hoped that they would help him convince Sean that April was still alive. Sean had also not called about the quilts and this angered Gordon, but he understood that Sean would be loath to contact Nora Epstein again if he thought that Gordon was ill.

Gordon began to haunt the archway into the garden and spent more time in the cold weather than was healthy for him, hoping for a glimpse of April, wherever she was in Dreamville. How had she discovered the corresponding places in Dreamville to those in her quilts? He did not know of the one in the window in the yellow bedroom, but he knew of the churchyard and the burn.

Damn it, Sean. Call. He needed to know the descriptions of the other sites at Burnock. He might be missing her just because Sean would not get the information for him.

Just as he was about to call Sean, the phone on his desk rang and he heard Sean's secretary tell him that Sean had a burglary to investigate and then would be coming by Burnock afterwards. She told Gordon it might be several hours, but that Sean wanted him to know he was coming by.

Gordon took that as a good sign and decided to go upstairs to see if Ian had woke up from his afternoon nap.

As he entered the bedroom, he was shocked to see April's reflection in the mullioned window. He rushed to the window and whispered her name.

She smiled at him, looked into the darkness behind her and then turned back to him.

She was crying and she looked as if she had been for a while.

"April, has he hurt you? Are you alright?"

She shook her head and wiggled her fingers at Ian who waved back at her from his crib.

"I miss him. I miss you. I sit by this window as much as I can hoping that I'll see him or you, but you've never seen me."

Gordon put his hand to the window pane and felt a liquid movement beneath him fingertips. April placed her hand against the pane on her side and for the first time in over a year they touched one another. Gordon was so full of grief that he almost fell backward from the window, but he somehow managed to stay keep his fingers touching hers.

"Oh God, April, can you come through this way? Could I come to you?"

Again she shook her head.

"No, don't try. I think the difference in the space, the small panes on your side might make it dangerous. I really have no idea what would happen, but something tells me it would be bad, like trying to climb through the burn."

Gordon still did not release her fingers and actually pushed his fingers through the small pane so that he could twist his fingers around hers wherever she was.

"Then how can you come home? How can I help? I can't bear to see you and not hold you, not bring you home."

She began to tell him everything she knew about what she knew about Dreamville or the dimension that she was in. She told him about Charlotte and how Will had murdered her, taken April's jewelry and put it on Charlotte's corpse and then had somehow moved through the window downstairs into Scotland.

"Can you use that window to come home?"

The tips of April's fingers came through the Burnock side and squeezed Gordon's hand.

"Oh, God, Gordon. I wish I could. That way seems almost dead now. Besides, Will put up shutters and locked them. But don't give up, there have to be other places that the two worlds touch that aren't dangerous to either of us."

Suddenly, Gordon saw her turn to look at the dark room behind her. She held his hand as tightly as she could and he did the only thing he could do – he leaned down and gently kissed her fingers and brushed them against his cheek.

"My love, use the quilts and look at Burnock. There have to be places that I can come home through."

She pulled her hand back from him and just placed it one last time against the almost liquid pane separating them, her hand resting one more time against his.

"He's back. I have to put the room back in order so he doesn't know that this window connects to home. Keep looking, my Scotsman. I need you. I need our son."

She stepped back away from the window and the small pane on the Burnock side became blank with only the view of the Highlands showing beyond it. She was gone like a ghost.

Gordon placed his hand on the window once more and felt nothing but the cold mullioned glass. He hung his head in despair and felt as if he might never see or touch his love again.

It was a great surprise to him when he felt a hand on his shoulder and he whirled around, not quite knowing whom to expect. Sean stood behind him, his face drained of color and sad.

"I'm so sorry, Gordon. I should have believed you. I can't believe that she was there in the window. I can't believe I could hear her or see her hand touch yours through the glass."

Sean sat on the foot of the bed and stared at the window.

"How? How can this be?"

Gordon still stood at the window trying to wish April back into his sight.

"I don't know Sean. There's so much about life, about our universe, about science that we don't know, that we may never know. All I do know is that she's alive and that that monster has her somewhere in that place she calls Dreamville."

He turned to Sean and remembered the tasks Sean had been supposed to have done.

"The exhumation. It was Charlotte, not April?"

Sean nodded his head, still dazed by what he had witnessed.

"It turns out that a woman from London named Charlotte Clarke had disappeared about six years ago.

Scotland Yard is treating this as a murder as there were knife cuts on her rib cage as if she had been stabbed. But the wounds were old. I doubt if they'll do much to pursue it."

Sean looked up at Gordon with a worried glance.

"Gordon, you can never mention Charlotte again. They might think you did it. They might even think that you've done the same to April. I heard April's account of how Charlotte died, but it would be impossible to get them to believe either of us."

Gordon nodded and sat down in the rocker next to Ian's crib.

"Did you call the Epstein woman? Did she have any information of the Pieces of April show? God, what a macabre name. As if pieces of her were spread across time and space.

"She's emailing me a copy of the brochure with the photographs of the quilts and the names of their owners. You own one, by the way. It was delivered to your home in Manhattan. Do you remember it?"

Gordon nodded.

"It's the only one. April said the others didn't seem to connect to ways home that were safe except for the Arch into the garden, one called the bench, also in the garden, and one of the kitchen trestle table."

He rubbed his temples and could feel himself getting dizzy.

"I need to eat something, Sean. I forgot about lunch when I saw April in the window. Now I believe my blood sugar had dropped. Come down to the kitchen. We'll have a sandwich."

He stopped and stared down at Ian again.

"Sean . . . would you mind? I don't want to chance falling on the steps with him in my arms. Mrs. MacCurdy will take over downstairs."

Sean smiled and lifted Ian up into the air.

"He's no longer the wee bairn he once was. He'll be running through the house soon enough and you'll have your hands full. I think you're going to need a nanny soon."

Gordon did not turn back to face his friend, but his tone conveyed how he felt about that idea.

"His mother will be back before then. No nanny."

Somehow, Sean knew that Gordon's face was dark with anger and determination. And now that he had seen April himself, he could understand why Gordon refused to give up. If he loved a woman the way Gordon loved April, he would do the same.

Chapter Twenty-Nine

April had just finished wiping the fingerprints from the glass and was sitting in the Windsor chair when Will opened the door to tell her that supper was ready.

She smiled slightly, lowered her head and began to follow him when he suddenly stopped in the hall and walked back into the bedroom.

"Something's different in here. I can tell. What have you done?" he asked as he pinched her left shoulder hard.

"Nothing. Nothing Will. I was just waiting for you. I wasn't sure about what to wear and I did go through the clothes . . ."

"Your clothes," he said interrupting her.

She nodded. "Yes, my clothes. I wanted to please you. Please, Will, you're hurting my shoulder."

He looked around the room. Something felt wrong, but he couldn't put his finger on it. He looked at her and she was dressed in clothing that had belonged to his Pamela, clothing that somehow she knew he had chosen. The dark skirt was shapeless and baggy and the matching dark green sweater almost two sizes too large.

"Will, I'm hungry. I know you don't want me to eat much, but I need to eat supper at least. Please? Can we eat?"

She lied. She had no appetite. All she wanted was on the other side of that window in that bedroom.

They sat in silence at the dinner table and at one point he held up his glass of chardonnay and stared at her.

"You've been thinking of them, haven't you? I can tell. You know you can't hide anything from me."

She began to be frightened by his words, but tried to hide it. What would be next? Would he lock her in a windowless room? The nightly visits with her son were the only thing that kept her going.

While these thoughts passed through her mind, he was swiftly around the table and had her by her shoulder, pulling on it so hard that she felt he might dislocate it. He dragged her down the hallway to the bathroom where he had murdered Charlotte and she began to pull away from him, begging, "No, Will. Please, no."

He used his free hand to turn the taps on the bathtub on then lifted her fully clothed into the quickly filling tub, pushing her down into the water.

She could feel the weight of the water sucking her down into the tub as he pushed her chest with all his strength into the water. She was crying out for help and begging him to stop, but no one came to assist her.

Soon the water was beginning to cover her face and she held her breath and she struggled to raise her face from the warm water. Finally the tub was full and Will pushed her under the water and held the upper half of her body there as her arms grasped for purchase on the slippery porcelain and her legs kicked against the end of the tub and the wall.

After almost 15 seconds that seemed like an eternity, he grabbed what was left of her hair and pulled her head from the water.

"They are gone! They are dead to you! If you think of them anymore or try to leave, I will kill you and nothing will ever take you back to them," he said and pushed her back under the water.

She had barely been able to get her breath when she found herself submerged again. But this time, just as she was about succumb to the water, through the water she saw a shift in the room. She saw not Will or his downstairs bath, but instead the white bathroom of her bedroom at Burnock. It was home. She relaxed her body and smiled. She could rise from the water and be home. All she had to do was climb from the tub.

Unfortunately, the smile broke the sadistic torture Will was forcing upon her and he lifted he from the water and unknowingly pulled her back into his world. He put her in the floor next to the tub and watched her to see if she was still alive.

When she saw that she was back with Will, she screamed louder than she had ever thought she could. She curled into a ball on the cold floor and could not stop crying. She had been home. Only the water had been between the worlds and the bastard had dragged her back into his world.

Will saw that she was alive and for the most part unharmed. He did not know that her tears were not from fear but from sadness and anger. He jerked her to her feet by the collar of the soaked sweater and pushed her up the stairs to the bedroom. Shoving her into the room, he took the key and locked her inside it.

"Too bad you didn't get to eat. Behave or you'll see much worse."

April heard his footsteps moving down the steps and she crawled over to the window. She was so weak from her struggle with Will and his almost drowning her that the distance to the window seemed so far away.

By the time she reached the window, some of strength had returned. She pulled herself up and looked through the windowpane for her family. At first she saw nothing and then the glass began to waver and lighten and there was Ian being held by Gordon as if they had both been waiting for her.

At Burnock, Gordon could see the condition April was in and he was truly frightened for her.

"April, what happened?"

She sat in the Windsor chair and could stand no more and in her real world, Gordon sat down with Ian on his lap and listened as she barely managed to get out the story of what had occurred. She had to stop at times to cough, still feeling as if water was in her chest.

"The Tub quilt passage is out. Now we know that,"

she said. "And probably anything that involved water. I was almost dead when I saw Burnock. I tried to climb from the water, but Will pulled me out of his bathtub just as I thought I was almost home. But now I think I was dying. My chest still burns from the water. I'm afraid if we tried the tub or the burn or even the sea that I would might die in the transition from here to there."

Gordon shook his head.

"There has to be another way, then. There are at least three that you haven't found that seem safe, almost like real doorways – the trestle table quilt, the garden bench, and the arch quilt. One of them has to be the way home. You need to find the door on that side and let me know. I'll meet you there and wait for you. Hell, I'll come there if I have to."

Ian clapped his hands and leaned against the watery surface of one of the small panes. His tiny hand slipped through and April quickly took it in hers and gently pushed it back to Gordon's side, but she could not release it. She had not felt his soft skin in so long that she could not stand the thought of letting go.

"No, Gordon. You have to stay at Burnock. You have to stay for Ian."

"Listen, April, Sean agrees with me. I might need to come to you to bring you home."

"Sean," she said. "How does he know? Did you tell him?"

Gordon sighed.

"Yes, Sheila and Andrew and I all did, but he didn't believe me. At least not until the last time we talked. He came to the doorway and heard and saw our entire conversation. He believes me now, especially since it was Charlotte's bones in the grave. DNA."

April reluctantly let go of Ian's fingers and he began to wriggle in Gordon's arms, trying to get back to his mother. Gordon, knowing the possible danger of the window, put him in his crib where the little baby boy began to cry.

"I don't care what Sean says. Gordon, you can't leave him. Don't be afraid of what might happen to me. Ian has to have one of us. Eventually, if I can't find my way back, he'll just think I went away. But he will always need you."

"April, love, I can't ever, and he won't ever get over not having you in our lives. We'll find a way. I know I swear it to you over and over, but we will. I'll wait for you again tomorrow afternoon here. If you've made any progress, we can discuss it then."

"Promise me you won't give up. Promise."

April touched the glimmering surface between them as Gordon reached up and touched her fingertips, too.

"I promise, Gordon. Just promise me you won't leave Ian alone."

He smiled and nodded. "I promise." As he said the word promise, the glass became solid, April disappeared and he was left standing with his hand placed on the small windowpane.

Chapter Thirty

Two long weeks of searching and long and painful talks with Gordon were beginning to wear at April's hope. She would love him forever, but she knew she might never actually touch him again, feel his body next to hers at night and those thoughts constantly chipped away at her hope and her strength.

It was at one of the torturous suppers with Will that she finally saw her way home. As his housekeeper brought in a bowl of broccoli and another of boiled potatoes, she held the door open with her foot and April saw Mrs. MacCurdy sitting at the long kitchen table at Burnock having her tea. She wanted to jump up and run past the woman because on the other side of the door.

She grabbed to the sides of her chair to hold herself in

place. Finally, after all this time, a way home. She needed to tell Gordon as soon as possible, but she knew that if she did not follow through the evening meal with Will that he might think someone was going on. She couldn't risk it.

That night she expected him to go out as he did almost every night, but he did not. He was in a jovial mood as if he had finally won the battle for April against Gordon. And so he led her into his living room and poured snifters of brandy for both of them. He chatted about this and that, but April could not or would not hear his words. She nodded and smiled and said "Really? That's interesting," when called for as if she were at a particularly dull party and was trying to be polite to the dullest man there.

She could not close her eyes and think of Gordon or Ian. All she could do was pretend. It seemed that she had never been so anxious to escape Will's presence as she was that night.

When he finally allowed her to retire for the evening, he leaned in and whispered, "I left something special for you upstairs. Just a little reminder. Then we can renew our marriage as it should be. A few more days and we will be together again."

She could feel and smell the hot breath of alcohol next

to her cheek and she pulled away, nodded at him and forced herself not to run up the stairs to see if Gordon was waiting at the window.

She could take it no longer and ran into the bedroom, where the first thing she saw was not the window, but a portion of the Chapel and graveyard quilt hanging from the ceiling, blocking her progress into the room. He had destroyed her work. He had cut away great sections of it and in other places had shredded the scene with long rips from scissors that in some sections allowed the batting to spill out.

He had only left one thing intact and it was not something she had sewn into the quilt. He had either added it or had someone else do it. It was the headstone that they had seen Gordon kneeling before and it bore her married name, April Stewart.

She ripped the remnants of the quilt and stuffed it into a trash can in the corner. Damn him, she thought. Putting April Stewart on the stone was his way of telling her that she was dead to those she loved and now she was Pamela only. She wanted to scream, but she knew that would only bring him upstairs and that was the last thing she wanted.

Running to the window she saw nothing but the street

outside and she sat in the Windsor chair fearing that she had lost her chance to tell Gordon of the kitchen door.

Will walked in as she sat in the Windsor chair, feeling defeated but not lost. He did not know what was driving her feelings and he thought his little trick with the quilt had brought her to this point. He was still drinking and he strolled across the room to where she sat.

"You'll love me now and you'll forget them as they have forgotten you." He leaned closer down to her, his face disgusting to her. She had never hated him so much as she did that moment. He sat the glass down on the table and began to grope at her breasts and push his tongue into her mouth. She fought him as hard as she had when he had tried to drown her.

And that was when Gordon appeared on the other side of the window. He called her name and he called Will's name in frustration, trying to get the man off his wife.

"Oh ho! I see I was right. You did have a secret in here from me. Well, he'll never get to you. I can see the room he's in and he can't pass through that window."

Gordon stuck his hand through one pane and tried to grab Will but failed.

"Gordon. The trestle. I found it. Go there!" she

screamed and kicked Will hard in the groin. She knew she wouldn't have much time to get away from him, but even a momentary pause would give her more time. Will bent over in what must have been agonizing pain, but still stumbled after her as she ran from the room.

"Run, bitch! I'll kill you for this. You lying whore!"

April was almost at the dining room door when she felt Will's hand tear at her blouse, trying to pull her back to him. She turned and tried to knee him in the groin again, but this time he moved sideways and avoided the blow.

He grabbed her hair and she turned again to face him, thought this time she took his hand next to her face and bit so deeply into it that she could taste the coppery taste of his blood as it dripped onto her face.

He grabbed his hand and started to curse her again, just as she threw open the kitchen door, praying that the transit would be open and that Gordon would be standing there, waiting for her. She saw him and was almost in his arms when Will tackled her, knocking the silver cabinet over, the silverware falling from the velvet lined drawers all over the floor.

No matter how much she kicked at him or pushed against him, he made his way on top of her and tore her skirt away from her bare legs. She looked up and saw Gordon's blue gray eyes and realized that this was what the horrible vision of Dreamville had been all along – not Gordon killing her, but watching her being killed, seeing his face as the last thing she would ever see on this earth.

And so she screamed as Will tried to take her there, scrambled her fingers for any piece of the silver and just as he was about end her life, she took a Sterling Silver meat fork and stabbed his throat with it.

He fell backwards, clutching his throat, unable to make a sound as his bright red blood sprayed across the dining room.

April pulled her skirt back around her and ran through the doorway into Gordon's arms. She clung to him and watched as Will's body ceased its writhing and lay still on the floor.

And just as quickly as the doorway to her home had opened, the doorway to Dreamville closed, this time forever.

They stood at the vanished portal and clutched one another as if Will would reappear and try to drag her back. They were in shock that the last ten years of the havoc he had wreaked on their lives was over.

"Oh, April, my love. I can't believe you're home, that you're really next to me and not a dream."

April buried her face in his chest and felt his heartbeat. She placed her hand over his heart. She had been lost and now she was found. All the rest would have to be explained somehow, but right now it didn't matter.

She tilted her head upwards and kissed her true husband and knew that all that mattered that she was finally and forever home.

ABOUT THE AUTHOR

Reneé Porter is the author of the series of novels, The **Taliaferro Chronicles**, including *The 13th Victim, Redemption Ridge*, and *An Inquisition of Angels,* as well as the novel *Bell Park.* **The Dreamville Trilogy** includes *Dreamville, Gordon's Dream,* and *Pieces of April,* the final novel in the series. *Pieces of April* is the author's seventh novel.

www.ingramcontent.com/pod-product-compliance
Lightning Source LLC
Chambersburg PA
CBHW070855250626
47159CB00003B/1071